DEFENDING BRIDGET

PJ FIALA

ROLLING THUNDER PUBLISHING

COPYRIGHT

Printed in the United States of America

First published 2021

Fiala, PJ

DEFENDING BRIDGET / PJ Fiala

p. cm.

1. Romance—Fiction. 2. Romance—Suspense. 3. Romance - Military

I. Title – DEFENDING BRIDGET

Paperback ISBN-13: 978-1-942618-56-0

DEDICATION

I've had so many wonderful people come into my life and I want you all to know how much I appreciate it. From each and every reader who takes the time out of their days to read my stories and leave reviews, thank you.

My beautiful, smart and fun Road Queens, who play games with me, post fun memes, keep the conversation rolling and help me create these captivating characters, places, businesses and more. Thank you ladies for your ideas, support and love. The following characters and places were created by:

Bridget's son (Axel's) Aidyn - Karen Cranford LeBeau

Bridget's mom - Vivian - Terri DeMario

Axel's nickname for Bridget - Irish - Nancy Hoch

Bridget's gun range - Armed and Dangerous - Kim Lowe Charlton

Restaurant on the outskirts of Lynyrd Station - Daggett Winery and Restaurant - Melissa Marie

Small Town in Texas where Axel grew up - Roarke Tx - Arlene Miklovic

Ukrainian buyer of girls - Mikheil Ustymovych - LeighAnn Fender
Ukrainian accomplice - Fedir Bulikov - Judy Gagliardi Wagner
Ukrainian accomplice - Viktor (Wiktor) Boyko - Wioletta Slyk
American who works with the Ukrainians - Kash Elliott - Kathy Franklin
Kash Elliott's sister - Angel Elliott - Jo West
Bar where Fedir is found - No Name Bar & Grill - Elena Pietrantonio
Town outside of Minneapolis - Carlsford, MN - Jenny Brandenburg

Skye's friend - Riah - Julie Collier
Yvette's friend - Bethany
Megan's friend - Carrie Gordon - Melissa Hultz
Bridget's clients Sydney - Laura Reinke Wagner
and Jennie Lee - Jennie Lee Ersari.
Bridget's friend in law enforcement - Kevin, codename Cobra - Mechelle Hopkins Hypes
Jax and Dodge's babies - Girl Maya/ Boy Myles - Belinda Jackson Hercule
Kerry Harteker - Medical assistance

A special thank you to Marijane Diodati, my amazing editor and Yvonne Cruz my proof reader!

Last but not least, my family for the love and sacrifices they have made and continue to make to help me achieve this dream, especially my husband and best friend, Gene. Words can never express how much you mean to me.

To our veterans and current serving members of our armed forces, police and fire departments, thank you ladies and gentlemen for your hard work and sacrifices; it's with gratitude and thankfulness that I mention you in this forward.

DEFENDING BRIDGET

Axel Dunbar was devastated when his former girlfriend aborted their child. Needing an outlet for his anger and frustration, the Army became his salvation. Eight years later GHOST came calling and Axel jumped with both feet into the murky world of cleaning up others' dangerous situations.

Bridget Barnes was Army strong and an expert markswoman. Now she's a wounded veteran. After a chance encounter with a sexy stranger left her pregnant, and locating her baby's father proved fruitless, Bridget set about being the best mom she could be. A meeting with a friend five years later brings her face to face with the man she never thought to see again.

With a madman bent on revenge against the GHOST team, Axel's world is thrust into chaos as he fights to save the son he's only just discovered—and the woman he's come to love—from the evil that lurks all around them.

1

L et's stay in contact, join my newsletter so I can let you know about new releases, sales, promotions and more. https://www. subscribepage.com/pjfialafm

***

Chapter 1

Taking the electronic tablet the driver handed her, Bridget tapped the "Tip" icon, added a generous amount to the total, signed her name, and handed it back.

"Thank you," she said as she opened her door.

Traveling light, as this was a day trip, she had no luggage. She walked up to the beautiful, older, brick building on the outskirts of Lynyrd Station, Daggert Winery and Restaurant, and the heavy, oak doors with old iron handles opened before she reached them.

Blinking in surprise, she stepped into the entryway which boasted stone walls, stone floors, and substantial, wooden furniture with studded accents. Decorations on the long side tables featured candlestick lamps with ornate shades, metal bowls with engraved wooden balls and a candelabra or two situated on the corners.

It was all she could do not to murmur, "Wow."

"May I take your jacket, ma'am?"

She was flustered that she hadn't seen the man wearing black dress slacks, a crisp white shirt, and black vest with a black bow tie standing tall and straight as he waited for her to answer.

"Of course, thank you."

He helped her remove her jacket, folded it neatly over his arm, and asked, "Are you here for the Vickers' baby shower?"

"Yes, I am."

This all seemed so unlike Sophie, at least the Sophie she knew in their Army days. But she'd heard that she'd married into money, though she'd never have guessed this much. Then again, you never knew about anyone, right?

Suddenly feeling self-conscious and maybe underdressed, she looked down at her sleek, gray trousers and her soft, gray and white floral blouse and hoped she didn't stand out - in a bad way.

The waiter, or supervisor, or whoever, bowed slightly from the waist. "Please follow me."

He turned and she followed him into a room off to the left. The first thing she noticed was a wall of windows that looked out onto expansive gardens alive with varying flowers of every color, shape, and size. A tall wooden covered bridge graced the back of the property. The whole scene was picturesque and breathtaking.

A baby grand piano stood in a corner close, but not too close, to a tall stone fireplace. High above was a narrow wooden mantle and on top of that lay a bobcat which looked as if it were watching her. She stared for a few moments and realized it was a real cat, though no longer alive, but an expert taxidermist had beautifully preserved it.

"There you are."

She turned to see Sophie still as gorgeous as ever, maybe even more so, with her full rounded belly, glistening, long, dark hair and shiny brown eyes. Her smile said it all, this woman was happy.

"Oh. my God, Sophie you are simply glowing."

Sophie wrapped her in a warm embrace, and she reveled in holding her friend close. A slight thumping against her had her pulling away and she looked down at Sophie's baby belly.

"I just got kicked."

"You did." Sophie laughed. "She must not like all the activity today. She's been kicking up a storm."

"It's a girl? I thought you weren't going to find out before you had him or her?"

"I don't know for sure, but I enjoy calling her a her because Gaige would really like a boy and it gets him flustered. He said he wouldn't know what to do with a girl."

Bridget laughed. "He has nieces, he should know a bit anyway."

Sophie giggled, nodded and lay her hand on her belly.

"Wow, I'm so stunned, Sophie. You look...content and so beautiful. Pregnancy agrees with you."

"Oh my God, I'm so happy, Bridget. I can't even put it into words how elated I am. Marriage agrees with me. My job agrees with me and this,..." She lovingly smoothed her hands over her baby bump. "This definitely agrees with me."

Unable to resist, she pulled Sophie in for another hug as close as she could get and held on tight.

"I'm so sorry I couldn't make the wedding, but Aidyn was sick. I can't leave when he's not feeling well. He had a flu bug that lasted only a couple of days, then he was as good as new."

"How is Aidyn? What fun new things is he into these days?"

"He's great. He's growing up so fast. Lately he's into dinosaurs."

"That's fantastic. I hope you brought tons of pictures."

Laughing, she said, "You know I did."

Bridget pulled her phone from her purse, scrolled, tapped, and looked at the face of her little boy, so adorable and innocent. "Here he is."

Sophie took her phone and scrolled through her pictures. Her stunning smile and exclamations a tell as to how adorable she thought Aidyn was, too.

"Oh my God, he's getting so big. You must be so proud. He's just so precious."

"I am, always. He's a handful, but he's also mine. My mom says that he's just like me when I was his age."

"Moms have a way of doing things like that. I'm sure I'll be hearing similar remarks from my mom." Sophie turned, put her arm around Bridget and began walking them to another room. "Come on back and let me introduce you to my friends. They're excited to meet you. I've been telling them of some of our exploits while we were in the Army."

Bridget walked along with her friend, her hip not as sore today as other days, through this magical place and fought the feeling that they'd gone back in time. "I hope you aren't telling them everything!"

The glint of mischief in Sophie's eyes gave her pause. "Not quite everything. Some things should be left for us. And Kate. We'll keep some of our memories of Kate and our antics between us."

Wrapping her arm around her friend's waist she pulled her close as they continued to walk through a gorgeous sitting room furnished with large-scale leather high back chairs in front of yet another fireplace with a small table in between them. "I miss you both so much, Sophie. I was so devastated when I heard of her death. It broke my heart when you went missing for a while, I worried myself silly. I'm so relieved that you found Gaige again and that you're still with us. Between us, Kate will always be alive. At least here." She pointed to her heart and she meant it. Kate was just the best.

"If this is a little girl I'm carrying, I'm naming her Kate."

Bridget swallowed the lump that instantly formed in her throat. Blinking rapidly to stem the tears that threatened, she nodded, squeezed Sophie's waist, and whispered, "I think that's perfect."

2

Axel couldn't help but feel melancholy. At least a bit. He'd always wanted to be a father. Always.

"A father isn't something you want to be." One friend, Dick, teased. "An astronaut is something you want to be. You become a father when you get your girl knocked-up."

When his high school girlfriend, Donna, found out she was pregnant, he dropped his plans to join the military and found a job in his small town of Roarke, Texas. He figured that he and Donna would get married. After the shock of finding out he was going to be a father, he was happy about it. He was sure he'd be a good one. Four months later, he found out through a friend that she'd had an abortion. She was a coward. She just moved away so she didn't even have to face him. And that was the end of his new job. He followed his original plans and joined the Army the very next day. Devastated, he pushed being a father to the far depths of his heart.

Shaking the sad memory from his thoughts, he continued through the barn, the soft nickering of horses and the crunching of the fresh hay beneath their hooves filled his hearing and calmed him.

Running steps from behind him had him bracing. Josh caught up to him and slapped him firmly on the back. "What's it going to take to lift you out of this funk you're in?"

"I'll be fine, I'm just feeling sorry for myself."

"I understand they have a paintball field in the back of the barn and courses set up around the property away from the restaurant. Wanna play? Or should I say, Wanna get your ass kicked?"

Axel laughed out loud. "Fuck you, I can beat you blindfolded."

"Let's put it to the test, smart ass."

Running through the woods, shooting paintballs at his friends sounded like just the ticket to bring his mood back to its usual happy self, busting his friends chops.

Following Josh, who seemed a little too eager for fun and games considering they'd just come off a nasty government mission involving some major international arms dealers that nearly went south. But everyone had their own way of shaking off the hazards they'd faced during an operation and putting their minds right. His usually involved hitting the shooting range and firing off a hundred rounds or so. Then a hard workout, followed by a long nap. There was something about the smell of gunpowder, then sweating profusely followed by a hot shower and deep sleep. He usually woke, ready to go and eager to take down more vile scum.

He heard his friends and teammates teasing each other in the tack room off the barn and entered the room to see them selecting paintball guns and the colored paintballs of their choice.

Wyatt laughed and said to Gaige, "Isn't Sophie going to kick your ass when you go into the restaurant covered in paint?"

"Fuck you, I'm not the one going in covered in paint. That's for you losers."

Dodge looked over at Axel, winked, then shot Gaige in the thigh, leaving a big blue splotch on his jeans. Gaige howled as the paintball hit. At this close range, those little suckers hurt like a bitch.

"You just earned yourself an ambush, Sager."

Dodge laughed. "We'll see."

Gaige replied, "For the record, your wife is the one who will kick your ass if you go in soaked in paint."

Dodge laughed out loud and shook his head. "Yeah, Jax probably will. But the makeup sex is amazing."

Josh, Jax's twin, yelled, "Stop that. I don't want to hear about you having sex with my sister."

The room full of guys laughed. Lincoln shook his head. "You've seen her lately haven't you? She's carrying twins and looks like she'll have them any day now, so clearly, she's had sex."

Josh pointed his paintball gun at Lincoln, but Lincoln turned and ran from the room, out the backdoor where their guide waited for them.

"Chicken!" Josh yelled. But he quickly burst out laughing.

Axel's mood was already lifting. Yeah, this is what he needed, some fun with his friends, shooting, getting dirty and then eating a delicious meal. Today was looking up.

***

Axel and Gaige ducked behind the large rock they'd found for cover. This game required them to form teams. There was a flag in the ground on the other side of the deep ridge. Each team had to come out 'alive', which meant in paintball terms, not hit during the game. Axel looked over the top of the rock, his eyes scanned the uneven terrain, and he watched for the other teams. A paintball flew over his head to the left and he dropped down immediately. "Fuck. They know where we are."

"Okay, let's move out to the right. That Oak tree over there will provide us some cover."

"Roger. You go first and I'll cover you."

"Roger." Gaige crept low to maneuver to the edge of the rock. Axel looked around the right side of the rock and waited. Slowly pulling his gun up, he glanced around the area, then whispered, "Go."

Gaige took off running to the Oak tree, dove on the ground and made it just as a paintball whizzed by Axel's right ear.

Ducking behind the rock again, he situated himself to the side of the rock Gaige had just vacated, looked over at his friend, who had hunkered down behind the tree and was looking around. The rustling of leaves had him looking up over the rock to see Josh running for cover to a location across the ridge from them and taking fire. Using the diversion to run to the tree, Axel took off as fast as he could and slid on his heels as he ducked behind the tree, still alive.

Gaige smiled then patted him on the back.

Gaige's phone buzzed in his pocket, and he rolled his eyes, "We're caught for sure now."

Pulling his phone from his pocket, he whispered, "Vickers."

"Gaige, this is Mrs. Vickers and it's time to get back for lunch. What are you guys doing anyway?"

"We're playing paintball and you're going to get us killed."

"Well, I'll just say this, if you all make Jax wait another minute to eat, she'll kill all of you and you won't have to worry about being killed by a paintball. She's eating for three and she's hungry as a bear."

"Shit."

Axel laughed and shook his head. "Poor Dodge."

Gaige pocketed his phone, stood behind the tree, and yelled out to his friends and co-operatives.

"Dinner time. Dodge, especially you, your wife is starving and she's getting hangry."

Josh could be heard laughing the loudest but some of the other guys were laughing loudly, too. Then Josh stood first, hands up and said, "Calling it."

But, as guys do, rather than letting him just call the game, they each pummeled him with paint. His howls of pain could be heard over all the shooting, leaves rustling and laughing.

"I'm gonna get you fuckers."

Dodge stepped out from behind Josh, laughing. He slapped Josh on the back and shook his head. "Had to do it, bro."

3

Bridget sat at a small table with two other women, Skye Winter, who was married to Lincoln, and Megan Montgomery, who was married to Ford and tried desperately to remember everyone's names. She'd been introduced and wonderfully welcomed by all of these women but meeting everyone all at once made it harder for her to remember their names.

Megan leaned forward and caught her attention.

"What do you do for a living, Bridget?"

Finally, she had a topic she could talk about. Though, it was often frowned upon.

"I own a shooting range. I mostly work with women, training them how to handle their weapons, clean them, take care of them but mostly how to shoot them precisely and safely."

"That is so cool. I'm envious of you. Maybe one day you'll help teach me how to shoot."

"I'd love to. What do you do for a living?"

Megan laughed and she found herself being the envious one. She was gorgeous with her perfect teeth and long, auburn hair. Her skin was flawless, and her eyes were the greenest eyes she'd ever seen.

"I used to be a nurse, now I'm a stay-at-home mom of an almost two-year-old daughter, Shelby, and as you already know Ford's wife. Since they're schedules..." She motioned around the room, but mostly toward Jax, who was sitting in a chair, looking very uncomfortable, "are so unpredictable, it's impossible for me to work outside of the house. I'd never know when I needed daycare and for how long."

"I can understand that. I have a son, Aidyn, who'll be five in a few months, and I had to set a regular schedule with my business so my mom, who watches him, could have a life, too."

Skye looked at her. "Do you have pictures of Aidyn?"

Bridget pulled her phone from her purse and scrolled to her pictures. Finding the photo file of Aidyn, she tapped the first one and turned her phone.

"Oh, he's a good-looking boy. He has the prettiest hazel eyes I've ever seen." Skye looked up at her and smiled. "Must take after his father."

Bridget swallowed. "Yes, he does."

Skye passed her phone to Megan, who had similar compliments and Bridget smiled at the praise. Megan handed her phone over, and Bridget asked, "Do you have pictures of Shelby?"

Megan smiled. "Of course, I do." And proceeded to pull her phone from her purse, tap and scroll.

"Oh, gosh, I get it now. "Shelby, Ford. Haha, that's great."

Megan laughed, "Ford also has a son named, get this, Falcon."

The women all laughed as the door swung open from the back of the room and their group of men, covered in paint of varying colors and hues, entered. The women all grew silent and stared at them.

Jax was the first one to speak. "What the hell have you been doing?"

"Playing paintball." a man about Jax's age, who looked remarkably like her, with an enormous smile answered.

Jax sat forward in her uncomfortable chair and looked the men over. Skye leaned forward and quietly said, "Uh-oh."

"I can see you back there, Sager."

A tall, blond man with broad shoulders stepped forward a sheepish smile on his face.

"Hey, Little Mama, how are you three doing?"

Jax looked him up and down; though he wasn't plastered in paint, his pants were dirty like he'd been playing in the mud and there were leaves hanging from the back of his t-shirt.

"Geeze, I don't even know what to say. You make me mad, sad and jealous all at the same time. You're taking your clothes to Mrs. James to clean that mess up."

Dodge laughed and so did most of the other men, though they were trying to hide it.

Bridget leaned forward and asked quietly, "Who's Mrs. James?"

Skye responded, "She works at the compound and does everyone's laundry. At least those who live there, and I'm guessing, Dodge's."

The ladies at her table giggled and Bridget wondered not for the first time, what the compound was. Sophie had mentioned it before, too.

Sophie stood and walked over to a man, though he didn't have a ton of paint on him, had a few spots here and there. Taking him by the hand, she walked toward Bridget, Megan and Skye.

"Bridget, this is Gaige. Gaige, this is the infamous Bridget Barnes. Sharpshooter, entrepreneur and amazing mom."

Gaige had green eyes, a nice smile and he stood tall and proud. He held his hand out toward her and Bridget shook it.

"It's nice to finally meet The Gaige Vickers I've heard so much about over the years."

He smiled, but his eyes turned to look into Sophie's, and an instant pang of jealousy stabbed her in the heart. That look. The one Gaige gave to Sophie and Sophie returned. She wanted that.

Soon two other men came to their table and she was introduced to Ford and Lincoln. She watched as most of the other men wandered into the other rooms, presumably to clean up and not be yelled at.

Yvette, who she'd met earlier, stood next to a tall, very tall dark-haired man with tattoos everywhere and a beard called out, "Let's all go into the dining room and have lunch while it's warm."

The group meandered through the room, but Sophie and Gaige waited with her as the rest left the room, then they walked with her to the dining room. Just like the rest of this gorgeous building, the dining room was as opulent as expected. Long dining tables were decorated with black table linens. Gold and red centerpieces were placed every few place settings, candles were lit, and the room was romantic.

"Wow, Sophie, this place is amazing."

"It is. Jax talked me into having my shower here. She had her shower here last month and I fell in love with it. I probably shouldn't have spent so much money, but it's our first child. Plus, I'm trying to make up for some special people you know who won't be able to share this with me. Not that this makes up for Tate and Kate's absence, but for some reason, I wanted to make this so special, so if they're watching from heaven, they'll see I'm doing well. Does that seem stupid?"

"Of course, it doesn't."

Gaige leaned in and whispered, "Plus, you two are worth it."

He lovingly patted her belly, then kissed her nose. "Let's sit, I'm hungry."

Sophie giggled and took Bridget's hand. "Sit with me."

4

Axel splashed water on his face and raked his hands through his dark hair. He'd grown it out a few years ago since he was still a bit self-conscious about the scar that ran down the right side of his face. Wyatt had a matching scar on his left side they'd gotten from the same asshole they were trying to bring in on a mission five years ago. The suspect was high and went after Wyatt first; his scar was worse extending down his teammate's neck. He was afraid he'd lose his teammate. He'd jumped the guy and the knife-wielding suspect cut his face before he took the asshole out. Growing his hair long had women noticing his hair and not his scar. At least the few times he'd had an opportunity to meet a woman, but nothing ever transpired beyond meeting them. He worked so much it wasn't easy to meet women. Kind of hard to be a father when you weren't there. Life had a way of punching a person in the gut then laughing in his face.

There was a time he'd dreamed of a wife and babies and a regular nine to five job. He'd set his sights on that when Donna got pregnant. He'd dreamed of playing games with his kids and going to soccer games. But, those days were over.

Washing his hands, he grabbed some paper toweling and dried them off. Exiting the bathroom, he made his way to the delicious smelling food and the voices of his friends in the dining room.

Stepping into the dining room, he saw three tables set up in the room for their group and no other tables. Gaige and Sophie had rented the place for the day, just like Jax and Dodge had done last month.

Josh looked up at him as he entered the room and waved him over to sit across from him.

"Most everyone is paired up, except us and the smoking-hot redhead next to Sophie."

He tilted his head to the table across the room.

His eyes followed the direction of Josh's head and landed on her. The redhead. The one he had a hard time forgetting about all these years later. Looking away from her was almost impossible. She was still a knockout. Her shiny, red hair hung down over her shoulders. A slight wave of hair curved around her left cheek and created the perfect softness for her face. Not that she needed it. But, he knew from the little bit of time he'd spent with her that she was tough. Former military, self-assured, dauntless. Dammit, she was like a drug to him. And then she was gone.

"What, you know her?" Josh's voice broke into his thoughts.

His eyes moved from the softness of her hair to Josh's brown inquiring eyes. "Um, yeah. At least I think it's her."

"No way. How do you know her and how is it you know her but haven't claimed her?"

His eyes landed on Josh. "Claimed? What are we wolves?"

"I mean, what is she, batshit crazy or something?"

"No. I mean I don't know. I don't know her that well, I just met her a few years ago at a bar."

"Did you..."

"Knock it off." His eyes landed on her again. Same full lips. What he could see from the table up, she was still slender and delicate. But he also remembered a woman who knew what she wanted and expected to get it.

She laughed at something Sophie said and it was like a gut punch. Damn she was sexy. He could barely hear her laugh over the voices of his friends talking in the room, but what he could hear brought a memory crashing into him. They were sitting in the bar at the hotel both were staying at. He used a cheesy pickup line, something about falling from heaven and she laughed. Then she looked him square in the eyes, hers the prettiest green he'd ever seen. She leaned in and the fragrance she wore, citrusy and fresh, wrapped itself around him as her lips curved up in the most beguiling smile.

"Look here, handsome, I don't fall for stupid pickup lines. I'm not an easy mark. I don't even flatter easily. So, if you think you have a shot with me, you'd better bring, not just your A game, but your A plus, plus game."

He laughed and he remembered how her eyes watched his. He knew, in that moment she was smitten, and she'd be his by the end of the evening. He brought his A plus, plus game. He brought it over and over if memory served.

"You fuck with Sophie's friend and Sophie will kick your sorry ass."

Looking at Josh again, he grinned.

"Well, I haven't had my ass kicked by a pregnant woman ever."

Jax, who sat across the table between Josh and Dodge, leveled a scary gaze on him. His stomach tightened at the look in her eyes. She'd been rather testy lately, big as a house with twins, not able to work out like she used to and worried about what in the hell she was going to do with twins and how would she work. The decision had been that her mother, Pilar, would be moving into the wing they added to their home. So, Jax was stressed, pregnant and irritable.

"Today going to be your day, Axel?" she asked softly.

"No, ma'am." he replied. Then he thought he should soften her up a bit. He smiled at her and winked. That usually did the trick. Usually. Today she just stared at him, she didn't even move. He squirmed in his chair, twice and then she burst out laughing.

"Gotcha."

"It's not fair 'cause you're huuugg...pregnant."

"You almost got your ass kicked just now. You call me huge ever again and I don't care who's around, you're going down."

Tapping on a glass had them all turning toward the front of the room and Roxanne, Hawk's wife, as she called for attention.

"Thank you all for coming today to help us shower Sophie, Gaige and Little Vickers with gifts. These two, finally, and when I say that I mean FINALLY got their act together and tied the knot. Then didn't waste any time getting pregnant. So, we'll need to hurry and eat then open the gifts, 'cause now that they have their rhythm, they'll be moving fast."

The crowd in the room laughed and he couldn't help himself, he looked at her. Irish. That's what he'd called her. She said she had been the top of her class on the gun range and the only sharpshooter in her unit.

Just as he remembered her nickname, she turned her head and their eyes met. The bolt of lightning that shot through him intensified as it landed in his cock. She nodded slightly and he squirmed again, this time for a much different reason.

5

Bridget stood as they left the room. The lunch had been delicious, the gifts lavish, and she was thrilled that she'd opted for the one thing she thought no one would think of for a baby gift. She'd sent it ahead earlier this week to Roxanne, who was kind enough to bring it today. It was a collection of books for the baby, swaddles, and a sling for carrying the baby around when you just must get stuff done. She assumed no one else had gotten them anything like this, according to Roxanne, and she felt relieved when she sent them. She'd been very lucky that Sophie had mentioned Roxanne, the wife of Hawk Delany, who worked with Gaige. Sophie had told her about Roxanne's unusual silvery-white hair. She'd been spot on in her description.

Just as she made her way to the door to head out to the room where they'd first gathered for dessert, he was there. Robert Beckman. Butterflies came to life in her tummy as he neared her. His aftershave, which was so damned sexy, wafted over her and she remembered the night they'd spent together. Telling herself what a dirtbag he was though, she steeled herself against his charms. That damnable smile, his full lips, those hazel eyes. Dammit, that had been the first thing she'd noticed about him five years ago.

"Irish, I had no idea you and Sophie were friends."

She stopped just before exiting the dining room and he stopped alongside her.

"I'm going to go way out on a limb and say there are so many things you don't know about me it would make your head spin."

His brows came together, then quickly relaxed. The surprise at her words showed in his eyes for the briefest of moments before speeding off in another direction.

"Let's rectify that. Have dinner with me tonight and you can spin my head."

"I can't. I've got someone to get home to."

She saw his smile fall and the disappointment on his face. It felt good to disappoint him. She'd been so damned disappointed these nearly five years in so much about him.

"Fair enough." He then held his hand out for her to exit the room first and she raised her head, squared her shoulders and walked out to the rest of the shower guests who'd gathered around while Sophie opened gifts.

Opening them one at a time, she was once again relieved when gift after gift was different from her gift. Silly thing to worry about, but she worried just the same. Trying to exchange something from afar was a pain.

Feeling as though she was being watched, her eyes darted toward Robert many times. Each time she found him staring at her and each time she looked away quickly. A couple of times she saw his brows bunch and knew he was puzzled by her reaction to him.

She decided to find Roxanne to thank her for bringing the gift with her. Yvette's phone rang and she seemed quite upset by the news she'd just received. Voices lowered as Yvette quickened her pace to speak with her husband.

She whispered in his ear, though he had to bend down a fair amount for her to do that since he was easily 6'7" or so and Yvette wasn't nearly that tall at about 5'6". Wyatt's black hair next to Yvette's lighter brown hair was striking together, but the way he looked at her, the concern on his face as she told him what was going on and his gentleness with her was a marvel to behold.

Yvette held her phone in her hand and Wyatt looked over at the biggest man in the room who she'd been introduced to earlier as Hawk Delany. Roxanne then stepped up next to Hawk as they waited to hear what Wyatt and Yvette had to say.

Wyatt looked into Yvette's eyes, and she nodded.

"Yvette's friend, Bethany, has been kidnapped from the parking lot at the office where she works."

The group murmured and Sophie reached over and put her arms around Yvette's waist and hugged her close. Sophie said a few things to Yvette and from the way they chatted, and the other women swooped into console Yvette, she realized one of the other reasons why Sophie was so happy. She looked at all this friendship and support Sophie received. It was inspiring.

Sophie then looked up and glanced her way. She began making her way through the crowd and Bridget admired how graceful she was even with her rounded belly. Bridget had always felt huge and clumsy and anything but graceful when she was expecting.

"Hey there. I'm so sad for Yvette. She's very close to Bethany. I'll pray extra hard tonight that they find Bethany alive and well."

"I will, too, that's just terrible."

Bridget looked over once again at Yvette, who stood close to her husband. The worry on her face was palpable.

"Wyatt's daughter was kidnapped last year and we were able to rescue her. So, this really hits home now. It was a sex trafficking ring hellbent on destroying young women's lives and lead by Yvette's former boyfriend."

Bridget turned to look into Sophie's gorgeous brown eyes.

"Is he at it again?"

"No, he's dead."

"Oh my God."

"It's okay, Yvette killed him."

"Oh my God, what the hell?"

Sophie took a deep breath, then took her by the elbow and began walking them to the large fireplace in the corner of the room.

"He was bad, very bad. He would place false job ads on social media and lure these young women to meet him supposedly for a job interview. Then he'd have a colleague come and nab them. They were selling some of the women to individual buyers. They intended to sell Wyatt's daughter to a buyer. They also were selling them to buyers who took them out of the country. Yvette had seen her former boyfriend's laptop and they may have been selling whole groups of women internationally. And you can only imagine what happened to them after that. We weren't able to find the few women Yvette believes they'd kidnapped previously, but we did find Dani, Wyatt's daughter and she's now in the military. She's going to save the world one day."

"I'm so happy you were able to save her. But is this starting all over again?"

"I don't think so. Her ex is dead, and his cohorts were captured by police. So, it's likely just a bad coincidence. We will watch this closely and we can work with the local authorities in Florida to get intel and make sure it isn't starting up again."

"Okay. How awful for all of those women."

"Yes, it sure is." Sophie held the side of her tummy and winced.

"Are you okay?"

"Yes, it's just that she gets restless after I eat sometimes."

"Here, come on over and sit down."

She guided her friend to one of the leather wingback chairs across from the fireplace and Sophie let out a long breath, then went into slow steady breathing to ease the pain.

After a couple of minutes, Sophie's smile returned. "I'm fine now, she just needed to tell me of her displeasure with something."

"She's likely big enough to come out and is feeling cramped."

"Well, I'm ready whenever she is."

"Good to know. I can't wait to meet her." She smiled at her friend. "Or him."

Sophie laughed and it was good to see her friend happy.

"Soph, I should get home this afternoon. I can stay if you need me, my mom has Aidyn, so she can watch him."

Sophie laughed again. Waving her hand behind her, "Do you see all those people over there? Good grief, I barely have a minute alone as it is. I'll be just fine. You get back to Aidyn and I'll call you as soon as I have this little peanut. I'll expect you to come back here and meet her right away."

"It's a deal."

Bridget stood to leave and saw Robert looking their way.

"Honestly Sophie, why is he here?"

Sophie scooted to the edge of her chair and turned her head to see who Bridget was talking about.

"He works for Gaige."

"Him? Really?"

"Yeah. He's a great guy, Bridget. Why are you surprised?"

Bridget shook her head. "It doesn't matter, Soph. I better dash so I don't miss my plane."

Sophie stood with a bit of assistance from Bridget, they hugged tightly.

"I love you, Bridget and I'm so happy you came to my shower."

"I wouldn't have missed it for the world. Except Aidyn of course."

"I can't wait to meet him. Bring him with you next time."

Bridget's eyes darted to Robert, but she smiled at her friend. "Of course. I can't wait for you to meet him, he's absolutely perfect."

6

She seemed pissed at him. His mind sorted through their evening together all those years ago and he couldn't come up with one reason why she'd be pissed. He only knew her first name, so he'd never been able to look her up, something he'd regretted time and time again over the years. Sometimes, you meet someone, and they just fit you. Fit didn't seem to be the correct word, but he was at a loss for another one. She fit him. They'd laughed and joked and man, they'd had sex at least four times that night. He couldn't stop wanting her. Her lithe, svelte body so agile and somewhat demanding of him. She gave him what he wanted in terms of how they coupled. When he told her to climb up on him and ride him, she rode. But, she wanted her orgasm to come, too and one time he'd cum before her and she made him keep going till she was done. Just that, right there, set in his bones. He'd never before thought a demanding sexual woman was what he'd want, but the few opportunities he'd had since her, he'd refused. Irish, in one night, had become the measuring stick by which he would compare all other women if there'd been any.

The next morning, he had to leave early, he was on a mission and was expected for a drop-off meeting at 5:00 a.m. He'd told her that night he'd slip out while she was sleeping, but he'd be back for breakfast with her by 8:00. He got back to the hotel and she was gone. He'd wanted to get her name. Her last name so when his mission was complete he could look her up. But, there wasn't a trace of her when he returned to the hotel room. He asked the hotel staff what her name was, and, of course, they wouldn't give that information out.

Finishing his mission and arriving back at the compound he brooded for a while, then told himself it was just another miserable experience with a woman.

As Bridget hugged Sophie and said goodbye to the other women, he followed her through the bar area of the venue. There was a smattering of people sitting at the bar and soft music played in the opulent room. Leather high-back stools and plush carpeting kept the sound muted so that the soft talking of the bar patrons didn't waft about the room.

Bridget walked through the room and stopped at the doorway to speak to the doorman. He bowed from the waist and walked away. Bridget tapped on her phone a couple of times then tucked it into the small shoulder bag she carried. She turned and saw him watching her. Their eyes locked for a long moment and he started walking toward her. Her slender body looked amazing encased in the soft gray trousers and the pretty soft printed blouse. If a person didn't know better, you'd think she was a refined woman who lived in places like this one. Her hair gleamed under the soft overhead lights and the swell of her breasts as she breathed highlighted her sexy body. She was an hourglass defined. Her silhouette was perfectly showcased by the lights from the foyer as she stood staring at him.

Before he could get to her, the doorman arrived and helped her put her jacket on. He felt irritated that that man was doing what he wanted to do. Be near her. Let his fingers brush over her shoulders lightly.

He quickened his pace and reached her before she darted out the door. He nodded at the doorman then tilted his head, silently asking him to leave them. Grateful he caught the hint, Axel faced Bridget, his breathing seemed to come in spurts rather than normal, his eyes drank hers in.

"Are you sure you can't have an early dinner?"

"I'm sure."

"I didn't get your name."

"Of course, you did. You've already called me by that name."

"I didn't get your full name, Irish. I also didn't know you and Sophie were friends. As I'm thinking back on the information you did give me, you were in town for a girls' weekend with some of your former military sisters. I didn't know her then, but was Sophie one of those sisters?"

He watched the thrumming at her throat as her heartbeat quickened. The pulsing in her slender neck seemed like the only movement she made.

"Yes, Sophie, Kate, and three others. We've all remained close over the years. Well, except Kate. She was murdered."

"I know we were involved in finding her murderer. You being with Sophie, it's a small world then isn't it?"

"Yes, it is."

A male voice called out. "Axel, are you harassing Bridget?"

He turned his head to see Dodge and Jax walking toward them. Jax, thankfully, had a smile on her face.

"I'm not harassing her."

Bridget looked at Dodge, her brows furrowed and asked, "Why do you call him Axel?"

Looking at him she said, "Is that a nickname or something. You told me your name was Robert Beckman."

Dodge and Jax both burst out laughing and the look on Bridget's face almost made him combust into flames right there. If she could have killed him with her eyes, he'd be toast.

Her phone chimed and she brushed past him and out the large oak doors before his mind could process what had just happened. It finally dawned on him why she was so angry with him. He was on a mission. He'd given her a fake name. She thought he was a liar, regularly telling women his name was something other than his own to get laid and he'd have no complications later. He turned to follow her out the door and as he stepped out onto the large stone porch, he saw her drive away in an Uber or some other such car.

7

Inhaling and letting her breath out slowly, Bridget tried calming her frazzled nerves. Glancing down at her hands, the slight tremor irritated her. She fisted her hands then released them. What she really needed right now was a vigorous workout to get rid of this pent-up energy. If her mom could stay with Aidyn for a while longer, she'd take that run or she wouldn't sleep tonight for sure.

Turning her head, she glanced out the window, grateful the driver didn't have a need to chat incessantly about nothing. She hated mind-numbing banter. "How's the weather?" "Are you having a nice trip?" God it all irritated her. She'd been told on more than one occasion that she should lighten up, but she didn't have the luxury of lightening up. She was a single mother, a business owner and a homeowner. She had a plethora of responsibilities and no one to help her with them. Well, she did have her mom to take care of Aidyn, but she hated having to impose on her.

"Which airline do you need, ma'am?" the driver asked.

She turned to look at him, then smiled. She should at least try to be pleasant. "American, please."

He nodded, watched the signs that pointed them in the correct direction, then turned his head over his right shoulder to check behind them, and quickly moved into the right lane.

Glancing at the clock on the console, she quickly figured her timing to be a bit early, but that was fine. She couldn't sit there and talk to Robert, or Axel, or whatever his name was today. The lying bastard. How could she have not seen the signs from him? She'd had her head turned by his witty banter, sexy eyes, full sensual lips and the way her body responded when he touched her.

At first, he simply reached over and held her hand while they sat at the bar in the hotel lobby. The goosebumps that skittered up and down her body at his mere touch did something to her brain. It made her stupid. That's what it was. Stupidity.

Then he'd smiled at her and in his deep, sexy voice said, "You are without a doubt, the most gorgeous woman I've ever laid eyes on."

That made her stupider. She felt like such an idiot, falling for his smooth talk and sexy eyes except she'd put him in his place about the cheesy line telling him he'd better bring his A game. Obviously he was a player. She squirmed in her seat from the abundance of adrenaline racing through her body. She pulled her phone out and texted her mom.

"How are things going? I'm nearing the airport now. If you can stay for just a little while once I get home, I'd love to have a quick run."

She held her phone in her lap and watched as the driver maneuvered through the myriad of lanes. Shaking the irritation from her head, she felt bad that she hadn't tried to be nicer to him.

Turning toward him, she asked, "What's your name? I'm sorry I haven't been very good company."

He shrugged. "Greg. It's no matter. I can't tell you how many times a day I get asked how the weather is here or some other inane conversation. It's been rather nice."

"Nice to meet you, Greg. I'm Bridget. I know you know that from my profile, but formally, I thought I could at least introduce myself."

His smile was broad, his eyes pleasant and friendly. "Nice to meet you, Bridget."

Greg's eyes darted into his rearview mirror then his brows furrowed. Bridget turned to look at the outside mirror on her side of the car and noticed a white SUV behind them.

"Has that SUV been behind us for a while?"

"Since we left Daggert Winery."

Greg navigated his little Prius expertly through the traffic and handled the various turn offs to American with ease.

"You've brought a lot of people through here I see."

He grinned, quickly glanced her way then as if by habit, looked in his rearview mirror before watching the road. "A few hundred is more like."

Another look at the mirror confirmed that the SUV had followed them this far. She refused to let herself get creeped out because as Greg just said, hundreds of people came through the airport every day. It easily could have been someone getting on a plane.

Greg turned three more times then slowed his vehicle down as they neared the terminal drop-off point.

They were approximately five cars from the drop-off point, but a quick glance at the mirror showed the white SUV still behind them. Normally, she wasn't one to get overly nervous about things. She made a quick decision.

"Greg, I'll cash out here if you don't mind."

"I don't mind waiting to take you to the drop-off point."

His eyes were kind, and he seemed a bit nervous that she was unhappy with him.

Smiling, she said, "I'm trying not to be paranoid, but that SUV is still behind us and in case they are following me, I'd like to get out of here and lost in the airport. It has nothing to do with you, I promise."

He let out a breath and smiled. Grabbing his phone from a holder on the console, he tapped a few times, then turned his phone around so Bridget could sign the credit card statement.

Signing with her finger, she added a generous tip, then handed his phone back.

"Since I don't have luggage, this should be easy. Thank you so much."

She quickly opened the car door, exited the vehicle with grace and speed, then rapidly walked up the sidewalk to the check-in point.

A quick head turn to see behind her showed a dark-haired woman getting out of the SUV. Bridget entered the airport doors, walked to the nearest terminal and stood in line to check in. Taking another brief look as the woman walked in the door of the airport, Bridget noticed that she was wearing a white blouse, white slacks and white heels. Easy to spot with her jet-black hair and overlarge sunglasses.

The line moved fairly quickly, and the woman merely stood by the windows trying to act casual. Bridget tried not looking at her; she opted instead to use a mirror app on her phone to watch over her shoulder. Finally reaching the agent, she checked in and rapidly walked to her gate. Sitting with her back against the wall and close to the plane entry door, she kept her eyes open toward the corridor to see if she could spot the woman. She'd arrived at the airport early, so unfortunately she had to wait for some time. What she wouldn't give for a first-class ticket.

Her phone chimed a text and she immediately looked to see who was contacting her. Trying to stem the fear that was permeating through her body and so in need of personal contact, she almost cried when she saw a text from Sophie.

"Thank you for coming to my shower. I wish we had more time to visit, but I'm so happy we got to see each other.

Please come and visit when the baby is born."

Blinking away the moisture that gathered in her eyes, she looked toward the corridor. Not seeing the woman in white, she texted Sophie back.

"It was wonderful seeing you. Marriage and pregnancy agree with you. You are positively glowing, and I couldn't be happier for you. I absolutely will come and see you when baby is born."

Tapping send she looked over the gate area to see if the woman was close or there at all. Not seeing her, she tried to relax, though she doubted she'd be able to relax at all until she was home. Her phone pinged once more, and she read the response from Sophie.

"Are you at the airport now or already in the air?"

"I'm at the airport." Her fingers began to shake.

Unable to resist looking around, she spotted the woman peering around the corner of the wall in her direction. Her heart hammered in her chest and she swallowed a large lump in her throat. Not sure what to do at this point, she decided since Sophie's husband was involved in some sort of security business, she'd let her know what was happening in case something happened to her.

"Hey, Soph. There was an SUV that followed me all the way from the restaurant to the airport and a woman has followed me through the airport. She's now watching me. If something happens to me, please get word to my mom. She'll take care of Aidyn, but I want someone to know that I'm being followed. Please don't make a big deal about this. I just wanted someone to know."

8

Flopping on his bed at the compound, Axel tried to get over his frustration. He'd lied to her. It was for work, but he'd still lied. He also didn't know she was Sophie's friend. Of course, at the time, he didn't even know Sophie. What a mess. Bridget would probably never trust him again. He'd now spend the next year or more trying to get her out of his head. He'd somewhat managed before. Though no other woman compared to her, he'd at least stopped seeing her face as he entered her. The look in her eyes as she gave as good as she got. The sounds she made as he pumped himself into her and the moans she emitted when she came. Oh, how he'd thought about that over and over.

Now, every time he saw a woman with red hair he'd think of her. He'd remember her perfume. His fingers would itch to touch her skin.

It just wasn't fair. Somedays life sucked more than others.

A knock on his door dragged him from his thoughts and he hesitated to let anyone intrude on them, dark as they were.

"Yeah?"

The door opened and Gaige appeared inside his sitting area.

"Hey, got a minute?"

Sitting up, he turned and set his feet on the floor. "Yeah." Walking out to his sitting area, Axel plopped on the sofa and motioned for Gaige to sit down.

"So, what's up?"

Gaige sat with his elbows on his knees and his head bent down staring between his feet.

"So, my gut tells me something's up. First Yvette's friend is missing and now Sophie just got a text from Bridget that she's being followed. An SUV followed her car from the winery to the airport. A woman, who got out of the SUV, pursued her into the airport and has been watching her since then. We can't get there in time before her plane takes off and she texted Sophie she doesn't want anyone bursting onto the scene. But it's too much of a coincidence that this is happening on the same day."

His heartbeat sped up to a rapid drumbeat. It almost made him dizzy. "Is she safe?"

"She's a bit freaked out, but it doesn't appear the woman has a ticket to get on the flight so as soon as Bridget can get on the plane she said she'll feel better."

"We should go there. Who would be following her? And from the restaurant where Sophie's had a baby shower?"

"That's why I feel uneasy. One woman with loose ties to GHOST is missing and a second one with similar ties is being followed. I'm just giving everyone a heads-up that we may be in for something here. I'm not letting Sophie out of the compound. We have what we need inside."

"Yeah. Thanks for the heads-up."

Axel's head was about to explode. He could go to the airport and watch over Bridget. She should have been using the GHOST plane but had no reason to. Also, she likely didn't know about it. He'd go and just make sure. He could be to the airport in fifteen minutes.

"What time is her plane to take off?"

"I don't know. I can check with Sophie."

Gaige pulled his phone from his back pocket and tapped a few times. His phone chimed within a minute. "She's on the plane now."

"Did the woman follow her?"

Gaige tapped and Axel's gut twisted. She was going to be far away. He couldn't protect her.

"Yes."

"What plane? Where is she flying to? I can get to the airport or take the GHOST plane and land at Bridget's destination airport probably before she will in a commercial jet."

"We don't know that her imagination isn't playing tricks on her. After hearing about Yvette's friend, she could have gotten weirded out and saw a woman a couple times in the airport and assumed she was being followed."

"But you felt worried enough to say something and what would it hurt to make sure she's okay?"

"Why are you so worried about Bridget?"

Axel pinched the bridge of his nose and inhaled. "I know her. Knew her."

"How's that?"

"A few years ago, I was on a mission and I met her in a bar. She was there for a girls' weekend. Sophie was there. I didn't know Sophie, so I wouldn't have recognized her if I saw her. Anyway, all of the other girls had already left, but Bridget couldn't get a flight out until the next day."

"So, you..."

"Yes."

"Shit."

"Yeah."

Gaige's brows pinched together but he said nothing else.

"I should go to Bridget's destination and make sure she's alright."

"Let me go talk to Sophie and see what else she might know. For now, be on standby."

Gaige walked out the door and Axel paced in his room. He should have tried to get her phone number. He could ask Sophie for it. She might not give it to him. But she might.

After the fourth time around his room, Axel thought he'd jump right out of his skin so instead of taking a fifth lap, he decided to go downstairs and see who was around. If nothing was going on, maybe he'd go down to the lower level where they housed their gun range, workout facility, clinic and conference room, which was their command center. He could either workout or shoot some rounds. Either one sounded better than wearing out his carpeting.

As he closed the door to his rooms, his phone pinged a text. Reaching into his pocket, he pulled his phone out and tapped the message to open it. Reading the text, his heartbeat ratcheted up to a tempo hard to control. His fingers began to shake, his vision began to narrow and the words he was reading began to blur. This was bad, very bad.

Thankfully, the woman sat three rows ahead of her. It gave Bridget the chance to watch her. Her heartbeat hadn't returned to normal since the woman got out of the SUV at the airport. Luckily, it was only an hour flight home. It was doubtful that she would relax, but she could at least make a plan. She had a few friends who were in law enforcement at home, and that was where she'd start. A quick look at the overhead sign showed the captain still hadn't turned on the "no electronics" sign. Pulling up her contacts, she scrolled through her friends list and found Jesson. Her fingers quickly typed out a message she hoped would send before they lost internet connection.

"I'm in an airplane and on my way home. I think I'm being followed and creeped out. Are you able to pick me up at the airport? Arrive at 4:15 p.m."

Tapping send she slowly released the breath in her lungs and sat back in her seat. A quick check that the dark-haired woman was still sitting in her seat allowed her to relax further.

Her phone vibrated in her lap, and she eagerly checked the message.

"I can't today. We're in the middle of a missing person's case. Try Cobra. But let me know if he can't pick you up."

Sadness settled in her heart, but she quickly sent off a text to Cobra, whose real name was Kevin. He was a badass and could absolutely protect her. She knew so many of these men and women from her business. After the Army, Bridget had a dream of opening a gun range and teaching men and women, but primarily women, how to protect themselves. She started small, working part-time at a retail store, while still living with her mom. She saved every penny she made at the store and in her off hours, proceeded to find the perfect place for her range. Then she started one at a time, offering her services. At first she found a little range out in the country and offered open shooting to anyone. She'd meet clients there and teach them the finer points of using their weapons. Holding their weapons properly, loading and unloading their guns, ensuring the safety was on and never pointing their weapons at anyone. Then, they'd begin shooting.

Her business grew quickly as empowered women would tell their friends and they'd call and schedule appointments with Bridget. Finally, the day came when her mom told her to quit her retail job and grow her business. Scared, but excited, she did that. Within two years she had the money saved to buy her place out in the country. She built her range, and her classrooms and started teaching significantly more women. When concealed carry became legal, she saw her class numbers grow.

As she gained a following and her former clients still came out for range time and target practice, she saw some of the local law enforcement officers started to use her range. That's when the business really blossomed. The area women loved shooting alongside law enforcement and the officers enjoyed offering words of encouragement and little shooting techniques for some of the women. Win-win.

Sadly, she hoped she never needed to call upon these officers, but she was beginning to feel as though she'd need to call in a favor or two.

A text came in from Cobra and relief flooded through her.

"I can meet you."

Without thinking she looked up to see the woman looking back at her. Sliding her finger over the camera option on her phone, she raised her phone and snapped a picture of the woman before she turned around. If that woman was trying to intimidate her, she'd do the same in return.

Sending the picture to Cobra, she texted.

"This is the woman following me."

She then pointedly looked directly at the woman who had turned once more but this time she smiled at her. Clearly this made her uncomfortable because the dark-haired woman quickly turned her head and looked straight to the front of the plane.

Feeling rather proud of herself she texted her mom and told her she had a ride from the airport and not to bother coming to get her. The last thing she wanted was her mom and Aidyn in any compromising positions.

More passengers began walking to their respective seats and she felt somewhat relieved when an older couple came to sit next to her. Watching out the window of the plane as suitcases were loaded, she listened as the flight attendant began the rote safety precautions and how to put on your flotation device if they crashed in the water and the like. Since there wasn't a body of water between here and home, Bridget focused on what was happening today. First, one of Yvette's friends was missing and then she was being followed and now her cop friend, Jesson, said he was working on a missing person's case. Three strikes and you're out. Vigilance was her new way of life. At least until things settled down around her. She felt completely vulnerable without her weapon on her and she vowed that the next time she visited Sophie, she'd drive the four hours so she could travel with her safety device and not worry so much about the time she'd spend in the car.

A few chimes sounded and the fasten seatbelt and no electronic devices signs lit from overhead. The plane began backing from the terminal and she inhaled deeply and let it out slowly. She hated takeoffs the most, and her nerves already had been ratcheted up for close to an hour now and it was exhausting. Another hour and she'd be home. By the time she went to bed tonight, she'd feel safe and secure in her own home where she had plenty of protection around her.

Feeling as though she was being watched, she looked up at the woman one more time and had her photo snapped by the woman, who then sent her an evil smile that stretched across her face. So, they would be playing games through the flight.

10

The elevator ride to the lower level and the conference room seemed to take an eternity. How had he never noticed the slow pace of this elevator? It was maddening.

Finally reaching the conference room floor, there was one more below which housed their vehicles, he stepped from the elevator and turned right. Eating up the steps to reach the conference room he could hear the voices of his friends and teammates as he neared. Opening the frosted glass door, the first person he saw was a very pregnant Sophie, looking scared and uncomfortable.

Allowing his eyes to look around the room further, he saw Yvette, Skye, Megan, Roxanne, and the rest of his teammates, including Jax, who was due any minute now. He loved her as a person and co-operative, but he sure as fuck did not want to have to witness her giving birth to twins. Not now. Not ever.

Inhaling, he neared the conference room table, nodded to Gaige and waited for him to begin their meeting.

"Okay, here's what we have so far. Yvette's friend, Bethany has gone missing as of yesterday morning. We've recently found out that Skye's friend, Riah is now missing as well as Megan's friend, Carrie Gordon. And, Sophie's friend, Bridget, left the shower yesterday and texted Sophie that she was being followed. This is not a coincidence anymore. Someone is targeting people close to us. It could be to get our attention. It could be to piss us off. Both are working. What are your thoughts on this?"

Axel spoke first, "Soph, did Bridget get home safely?"

Sophie pulled her phone from her back pocket and tapped on it a few times. "I've texted her twice and she hasn't responded yet. Let me try once more."

His gut felt as though a gallon of acid had been dumped into it. His head spun slightly and then he chastised himself for being weak. He barely knew Bridget. Sure, they had a wild night in the past. What? Like five-ish years ago? Still, his reaction to seeing her yesterday was disconcerting. Maybe it was that she rejected him. She sure hadn't back in the day, but yesterday, what was it about her? She looked more beguiling than she had in the past. She had a confidence and a soft edge about her that made her even more appealing than she had been back when they'd spent the night together. And, if he were honest, it had always rankled that she'd left him before he could make it back to see her. After all, he'd told her he'd be back at 8:00 a.m. It was as if she purposely left before he came back. She must have gotten up soon after he left. The coffee pot had been used. She'd showered, dressed, packed and left all before he could get back.

"She just responded. She has a LEO friend who came to the airport and picked her up. She's home safe and sound now." Sophie read.

His stomach felt better except the part about the LEO friend. How close of a friend was he or she? He wanted to ask. But, that would seem rather weird considering there were three missing women right now. Mentally chastising himself he thought, "get your head in the damn game, pussy."

Lincoln spoke next, "I think we have someone bent on revenge. The most recent case we've had that involved missing women was Yvette's ex and his ring of sex traffickers."

Wyatt entered the conversation. "He's dead."

Ford then spoke, "Right, but his buyers aren't. What if they're pissed that we stopped their constant string of fresh women?"

Hawk added. "How would they know it was us? Who could trace anything back to us?"

Slowly all eyes wandered to Yvette. She saw the group looking her way and instantly plopped down into a chair at the conference table. Tears streamed down her face.

"I didn't say a word to anyone, but they could have my information from John."

Gaige then interceded to keep things rolling. "Right. So, let's say, it's likely that John told his buyers that he had you helping. Makes sense they'd want to know about you. Make sure you wouldn't squeal on them or somehow get weak in the knees about what was happening. Let's say, they didn't know what you knew. So, now that Caulfield is dead, and their stream of new women has dried up, they'd come to the one person they had a name and face for and somehow find where you are. You have a marriage license on record, so they could have tracked you that way."

Wyatt's hands rested on each of Yvette's shoulders, his fingers massaged gently as he spoke, "Okay, that's one theory, there must be others."

Ford entered the conversation. "Megan's friend, Carrie Gordon, was on her way home from work. She stopped at the grocery store and was carrying her groceries to the car when she was abducted. She lives in Chicago, Illinois."

Gaige walked to his computers, pushed a couple of buttons and a large screen slowly lowered from the ceiling.

"What's the name of the grocery store? I'll see about getting the video footage from them."

Ford looked at Megan and she texted someone while they waited.

Gaige asked, "What else? Skye where was Riah when she was kidnapped?" Changing the direction of his intense gaze, "Yvette, where was Bethany taken from? The women were texting people who could provide these answers. Maybe we'll have some commonalities we can begin with and I'll work on getting any video footage we can from the companies. If I have to, I can ask one of our contacts for help."

Axel's gut twisted and his mind screamed that Bridget was a target. He turned to Sophie, who sat looking uncomfortable and worry marred her beautiful face.

"Soph, is Bridget protected? If she felt followed, will she have someone to stay with her in case someone tries to break into her house?"

"I'll ask her. As far as I know it's just her and Aidyn at home."

His heart beat so hard he thought it would come through his chest. Aidyn? She had a man living with her. She said she had someone waiting at home for her, but he didn't realize they were living together.

11

W alking along behind the line of women, each one with their guns tucked into their chest at rest.

"Ready. Aim. Fire - two."

Observing them as she gave the commands, each one partnered up with another woman for class, watching to offer support and assistance.

The occasional instruction from one of the support partners could be heard. "Finger off the trigger," or "at rest." She smiled. There wasn't a woman here who didn't take this seriously.

"Ready. Aim. Fire - three."

The loud bangs were heard as each of the five women in line fired off their three shots. The little holes appeared on their targets as they hit them. Their shots, over time, clustered closer more frequently. Their aim better each week.

It was exhilarating seeing these ladies improve and learn how to keep themselves safe.

"Ready. Aim. "Fire - one."

Never really sure when the command would come or how many shots they would be required to take was part of the drill.

"Reload."

Watching diligently as each woman safely reloaded her pistol and stood at rest, she smiled.

"Ready. Aim. Fire - five."

The loud shots fired, and the air filled with the odor of gun powder. Bridget loved the smell of gun powder. A small smile crept across her face.

"Empty your guns, lay them chamber up in the case and switch positions."

A quick glance at the clock told her this was their last drill for the night. She hated that it was getting dark around 7:30 now. But, the deer were out, and she hated for these ladies to be driving out on country roads with the deer so abundant.

"Ready. Aim. Fire - five."

She continued walking behind the women to look for safety issues.

"Sydney, your gun isn't a teacup. Change your grip, please."

Standing behind Sydney, she watched as Sydney adjusted her grip, then smiled and resumed walking along behind the line.

"Ready. Aim. Fire - one."

"Ready. Aim. Fire - four."

She yelled out quickly not giving them the time to think about when the next command would come.

"Okay, ladies. That's it for tonight. You've all improved so much. Next week it's for all the marbles. If you graduate, you'll get your Certificate of Completion and can move up to the next level. Practice each night. Draw your pistol with no bullets in it. Safety first. Always. Use your practice bullets if you have them. Make sure your grip is perfect, you can rack your gun quickly and safely and practice your stance. Slightly forward from the waist. Butt out. Feet shoulder width apart and your right foot slightly back. You've got this."

Each woman emptied her pistol of ammo. There was no ammo allowed outside of this shooting range until they got in their cars. They could do what they wanted then. She watched each lady pull her magazine from her gun, position it in her gun case, lay her pistol in the case, close up her box of ammo and then remove her ear and eye protection and pack them up in her range bag.

One by one they waved goodbye and walked out the door. Bridget followed them out, and once the last lady left, she locked herself inside. Her house was only over the hill from the range and she had just enough time before dark to shut off the lights and close the lid on her computer. Working quickly, because she was still a bit creeped out by her experience at the airport yesterday, she hurriedly shut the light off, closed her computer and walked to the entrance. Pulling her keys out as she tossed her range bag over her shoulder, she opened the door slightly and felt relieved when she saw two ladies, Sydney and Jennie Lee, chatting by their cars.

She walked to her car, a wave for the ladies. "Good night, ladies. Don't wait too long."

"We won't." They called in unison then laughed.

Bridget got into her car, locked her doors and quietly started the ignition. Waiting for Sydney and Jennie Lee to get in their cars, she let out a sigh and eased her SUV from the parking lot. She watched in her mirror as Sydney and Jennie Lee then followed her from the lot. Feeling more at ease, she turned the corner that took her to her house. A quick check in her mirror and she watched each of the women drive past Mile Road, the road she lived on.

Inhaling and exhaling, she felt much better and would feel a lot better once she was locked in her house with Aidyn. Her mom had a bedroom in the back of the house usually for late nights, but she'd asked her mom to stay with her tonight, still a bit uneasy about the missing woman and then being followed. She'd call Sophie tonight and find out what had transpired with Yvette's friend. Hopefully, she'd just gone to a friend's house and was just out of touch. Hopefully.

Seeing her driveway up ahead, she quickly hit the button on the garage door, pulled into her driveway, turned around at the top and backed into the garage. It had been a habit of hers to do this. Always looking for the quickest escape if they needed it. Tapping the garage door button, she sat in her car until the door lowered to the ground.

Opening her door, she exited the car and entered her house, locking the door behind her. Safe at last. Arming both the security system at the range and the house, she turned to find her mom waiting for her in the kitchen.

"Hi, honey. Are you hungry? I made spaghetti tonight."

"Thanks, Mom, a small plate sounds fantastic. Is Aidyn already in bed?"

"Yes, he was exhausted. We played at the park today and then he had his soccer game. Those little kids are so danged cute running after the ball. None of them stay in their positions and those coaches have the patience of saints. But, he ran his little legs off."

Bridget smiled. That was Aidyn, running and playing and having fun.

"I'll go give him a kiss then I'll come back and eat."

Kicking her boots off at the laundry room, she quietly padded down the hallway to Aidyn's room. Pushing the door open silently, she stood and watched his little face, tucked so sweetly into his pillow, his breathing even and deep. That right there was her heart. Her whole life.

A sound from the front of the house caught her attention. Reaching back for her pistol, she pulled it from her holster and walked to the front windows. Standing to the side, she peeked from behind the curtains to see nothing in the front yard. Glancing around the landscaping close to the house a movement caught her attention. Her heart hammered, her breathing increased and her body stiffened. What the hell was that?

Bridget's mom entered the room and looked at her with her gun drawn. Her brows furrowed.

"What is going on?"

"I heard something outside."

Her mom, always levelheaded, walked to the window, cracked the curtain open and took a good look outside.

"It's a cat."

"What?"

"A cat. Running through the bushes."

Walking closer to the window, Bridget looked out the same spot her mom had and let the air whoosh from her lungs as the cat ran from under the bushes and chased after a bird.

"Oh."

Holstering her gun, she inhaled and let it out again.

"I think you need to tell me why you're so on edge."

_____

12

While they waited for their contacts to get back to them, Megan, Skye, Roxanne and Yvette sat around trying to pull together all the information they had. This would likely be a pro-bono job because no one had reached out to them. But, he'd gladly do it without pay to make sure Bridget was safe. He could at least do that for her. He felt connected to her, at least in a small way.

Skye read the text on her phone out loud. "Riah went missing from the parking lot at work. She worked in the morning but had a doctor's appointment in the afternoon. She left work around 1:00 p.m. But her car was still in the parking lot. The doctor's office called Riah's husband looking for her which prompted him to call her at work. Being told she'd left he drove to her office building and found her car still there. Scared, he called the police. They're investigating."

"Where did she work?" Gaige was pecking away on his keyboard.

"She worked at Insurance America, a large insurance company in Denver, Colorado."

Skye looked up at her husband, the two of them together were a nice-looking couple. As he looked around the room his pride bloomed in his chest. This whole group was a great looking one. Not that it mattered, but he'd heard others say it on a few occasions and it always made him feel inadequate. The long scar on the right side of his face made him so self-conscious. Growing his hair longer helped him feel less insecure about it but it didn't take it away completely. The fact was that when he smiled widely or laughed hard, the scar tissue tugged slightly, and his smile was slightly crooked. And he was a man who liked to smile. Just then Josh smiled at something Dodge said to him and the perfect smile and unmarked face on Josh made him want to hide in a dark room. The women always loved looking at Josh.

Yvette then received a text and she read it to the group. "Bethany was leaving work. She worked late and was taken from the parking lot. She worked at a medical clinic. In Mazzulla, Montana."

Gaige turned and looked at everyone, "Okay, we have Colorado, Montana and Illinois. Not to mention that Bridget was followed home to Steuben, Indiana. No states in common. So far, the only commonality we have is that they had recently left work. Likely not feeling threatened in parking lots feeling that there were other people around would offer a sense of security. Other than that, we don't have anything else in common except they are all women. All around thirty years of age. And all have a friend associated with GHOST."

Gaige worked on a map, circling the cities where each of the missing women had disappeared from. Sophie's phone rang and she answered it, while scooting to the edge of her chair, then standing. She walked to the corner of the room, where it was quieter, and as the rest of the group talked about possibilities it wouldn't inhibit hearing her caller.

She stopped walking to the corner and turned abruptly. Quickly walking to Gaige, her voice panicked. Gaige's concerned look had him standing to usher Sophie into a chair.

"Bridget's on the phone. Two of her clients were kidnapped last night after leaving the shooting range. They left in two separate cars but together they went to a local bar for a drink after class."

Gaige took Sophie's free hand in his. "What is the name of the bar? Are their cars left there?"

Sophie asked Bridget the questions and listened as Bridget responded. "The Last Stop. And yes."

Gaige entered the information into their software and Sophie continued listening to Bridget.

Axel tuned in to try and hear as much, at least of this end of the conversation, as he could hear.

"Are you and Aidyn alright? How about your mom?"

Sophie's back was ramrod straight as she listened to her friend. Her free hand now curved around her baby belly, rubbing lightly as she listened to her friend.

"Okay. What about your LEO?"

Nodding slightly as if she understood what Bridget was saying, Sophie swallowed and her eyes glistened.

"I know. Right now, my first reaction is to tell you all to come here. We can keep you safe here until we get this worked out, Bridget, would you consider it?"

The talking in the room slowly suspended as everyone waited to hear what Sophie was saying to Bridget.

"We have a plane. We can come and escort you and Aidyn and your mom. We have the room. We have the means. Please let us help you Bridget. I can't lose another friend..."

Sophie choked out a sob and Gaige stopped working on his computer and turned to face her. He picked up her hand again and held it in his left hand as his right hand softly swiped away a tear from her cheek. To see his gentleness with her confirmed how he'd be with his child. It was a sight for sure because the Gaige they knew was badass and tough. They all were, including Jax. It was really going to be something to see her with two babies. He smiled as he thought about it. Then his eyes darted to Jax, who sat looking totally uncomfortable and squirming in her chair to try and get comfortable. Dodge leaned in and whispered something to her, and she took his hand in hers and shook her head no.

Then Sophie's voice rose a bit. "What?"

She sat forward in her chair. "When?"

"No shit?"

She closed her eyes then opened them to look at Gaige, her brows high into her hairline, the tears she'd recently shed dried up and surprise clearly on her face.

"I don't even know what to say, Bridget. I'm speechless."

She listened for a while longer and everyone in the room was now silent. To say you could hear a pin drop was terribly cliche, but it was the only thing he could think of right now.

Then Sophie's eyes landed on him and held. Soon the others in the room began looking at him and his mind went completely blank for a moment. Bridget probably just told her they had spent the night together and that's why she didn't want to come here. She'd turned him down quick enough yesterday when he asked her to dinner. But, now she might be in danger, it was no time to be stupid. Though, it was likely because her boyfriend, Aidyn, didn't want to stay somewhere where he was. He'd better do a damned good job of keeping her safe then, or Axel would go and find him and make him pay.

13

"Promise me you won't say anything."

Sophie stood, then whispered to Gaige, "I have to take this privately."

"Hang on, Bridget, I have to move to a different location."

Bridget waited on the other end of the line. Her heart hammered in her chest. She'd never said those words out loud before. She'd never even told her mom about this. She'd actually planned to go to her grave never saying those words to anyone.

She swallowed the saliva that had gathered in her mouth and she walked into her office and softly closed the door. Aidyn was in his bedroom and her mom was helping him get dressed. Once she'd gotten the call from the police this morning, asking her questions about class and Sydney and Jennie Lee her mind had reeled with the events going on. She was sufficiently scared out of her wits since she'd been followed and now her clients had gone missing.

She'd have to have a talk with her mom and tell her to stay here for the time being. She would forbid Aidyn to leave the house; she'd simply die if anything happened to him.

"Okay, I'm in my bedroom now and can talk freely."

Sophie sounded winded, but she was likely walking as fast as she could and being pregnant, no matter how great a shape a person was in, she was carrying quite a bit more weight than she was used to.

"Okay. I don't know where to begin."

"Begin at the beginning. When did you meet him? Where? Why didn't you say anything?"

Taking a deep breath and keeping her voice low so no one would hear her through the door, she answered.

"Sophie, remember about five years ago when we had our girls' weekend in California? You and the other girls left, but I couldn't get a plane out until the next morning. I was in the bar in the hotel that night. I had just had dinner and wanted a glass of wine before heading up to my room. He was there. At the bar. The way he looked at me, God, he melted my panties with just a look. So handsome, strong. Powerful, even in a suit jacket. I can't explain it, I wasn't drunk. He was just so magnetic."

Sophie giggled on the other end of the line. "He's handsome for sure, but I guess I've never found him magnetic."

"Shut up. You've pined for Gaige for years, so you know what it's like. You know what it means to just meet someone and know they are different from all the others. Anyone else you will ever meet."

"Yeah, I do know that."

Sophie sighed on the other end of the line and Bridget smiled to herself. She was thinking of Gaige and all the years she'd pined away for him. Those two had such an epic, if not sad, love story.

"Anyway. Epic night. Epic. But the next morning I felt him get out of bed and quietly dress. He told me he was there on business and he had to meet someone to deliver a package. The way he said it, made me think he was probably married and sneaking out of the room to get home early. He said he'd be back, but I had this feeling in my stomach that he was lying. Then I watched him walk out the door and he had a guilty look on his face. And I felt like a fool. I'd been duped by a handsome, strong, powerful man. My kryptonite. I'd let my guard down and paid for it. So, I got up, showered, made a cup of coffee, packed and left."

"Oh, no."

"Right. A couple of months later, I found out I was pregnant. I tried looking for him, but he told me his name was Robert Beckman. The only Robert Beckman I found was a deadbeat. So, I had my baby and set out to raise him on my own. I'm only telling you this now, because I'm beginning to feel like I'm being targeted and if anything happens to me, well, you'll need to tell him."

"We will do anything we can to make sure you and Aidyn are safe, Bridget. We've got to get you here."

"If I come there, he'll find out. He'll be able to see Aidyn looks like him. Same eyes. Same hair. Same smile."

"Isn't it more important that you all are safe and not worry about that? And, Bridget. God, Axel needs to know."

"No."

"Why not?"

"No, I can't."

"Bridget." Sophie's exasperated huff on the other end of the line was understandable. But, by this point, she'd spent so much time chastising herself for having her one-night stand. And with someone who was in prison no less. And, she still didn't understand what Gaige's company did other than security or something, and she didn't understand how Robert or Axel or whoever, fit into that company. And, she wasn't about to bring him into Aidyn's life until she knew he was an upstanding man. Aidyn deserved no less.

"I can't Sophie. Not now."

"I hate having this secret."

"I'm sorry. I didn't mean to drop this on you. But someone needed to know in case something happens to me."

"That's what we have to focus on. I'm having our plane come to get you along with two of our guys to escort you here and make sure you arrive safely. I won't take no for an answer so don't bother. Spend the next couple of hours cancelling your classes for the time being. I'll call you in a few minutes with details. Pack your bags."

The line clicked and she listened to the sound of silence for some time before pulling the phone from her ear and then setting it on the desk. Her fingers shook slightly with all the emotion that was currently running through her body. Truth be told, she should go away for some time and get Aidyn somewhere safe. But being in close proximity to Axel was going to be difficult.

Her office door burst open and Aidyn ran in.

"Mommy, look what Gram got for me yesterday when we went for supper."

He proudly held up a colorful plastic toy and its top bobbed back and forth.

"That's wonderful, Bud."

"Yeah. And look, it does this too."

He shook the toy and it popped open. Aidyn giggled the most adorable little giggle and then turned and ran out of the room.

Huffing out a breath at the empty doorway, Bridget stood and decided she needed to have a talk with her mom while she waited for Sophie to call.

14

A xel set the free weights he had been lifting into the rack and flexed his hands to relieve the stiffness. Snagging a towel off the counter by the window, he scrubbed his face and neck with it and tossed it into the laundry basket.

Reaching for the door handle to leave the workout room his phone chimed a text from Gaige. Maybe there was news.

Pulling his phone from his pocket he glanced at the text.

"I need two guys to fly to Stueben and escort Bridget, Aidyn and Bridget's mom back here to the compound. Volunteers?"

While making strides to the conference room, just down the hall Axel quickly replied. "I volunteer."

He then continued walking toward the conference room. Entering the room, he found Gaige, Sophie, and Josh.

Gaige turned toward him when he entered.

"It's you and Josh. Pack up. Bridget has had two of her clients go missing from a bar last night after class. This is not a coincidence. Operate under the assumption that they couldn't get to her because she was protected, so they've taken women close to her instead."

"Is the plane ready?"

"Yes, I've called Gavin and asked him to file a flight plan. He's there and ready to go."

Axel looked at Josh who smiled, "Let's go get your redhead, Axel."

"We're off." Axel said and turned quickly to exit hoping Josh was following and wouldn't ask a ton of questions.

Heading quickly toward the elevator he jabbed the button that would take them to their rooms for a shower and their go bags, then they'd head down to the garage area. Josh's chuckle behind him told him he wasn't going to get away without the questions. He inhaled a deep breath and let it out slowly, waiting, rather impatiently for the first one to come.

Exiting their rooms less than fifteen minutes later, Axel and Josh stood once again at the elevator.

"I already know you know her. Oh my God, I can't wait to hear the whole story. And, believe me, I'm going to badger the fuck out of you until I hear it."

"Jesus," Axel muttered under his breath. Why did this fucking elevator have to be so damned slow?

Finally, the door opened, and he stepped in wasting no time in jabbing the button to go down to the garage. Josh hurriedly stepped in behind him, chuckling. "This is going to be good. I can feel it in my bones. Can't you feel it, Bud?"

"No."

That only got a large laugh from Josh and he knew, he just knew, Josh was going to needle the shit out of him all the way to Steuben. Son of a bitch, this would be the longest hour of his life.

Climbing into his truck, he stabbed the button on the dash and started the truck while a laughing Josh climbed into the passenger seat stowing the go bag on the floor.

"Still gonna ask you questions. Number one, who is Aidyn? You have competition for the redhead?"

"I don't know who Aidyn is."

Josh laughed. "Definitely competition. Probably a nerd, too."

Sucking air into his lungs till they burned he eased the truck up the ramp and out of the garage at the compound.

Luckily, as they exited the compound and rolled onto the street, Josh pulled the comm units from the go bag and readied them. His guts rolled a bit thinking they'd need them. This was supposed to be an escort mission and nothing more. But things could happen and often did in their line of work. Better safe than sorry, even if it was unnecessary. Hopefully, this time would be one of those safe don't need it kind of days.

Pulling up to GHOST's private hangar Axel was relieved to see that Gavin indeed was here and ready. The plane was already outside, leaving the empty hangar available for him to park his truck inside. Gavin was a valuable asset. Always ready to go, never asked too many questions and capable. Of course, he was paid handsomely, had military experience and understood what they did. He'd already had to fly into unfriendly territory to pick them up, under fire and he had never said a word about it later.

Parking his truck just inside the large sliding doors, Josh jumped out first and closed the doors. The runway was behind the hangar and they exited through the backdoor, locked it up and walked toward Gavin who stood outside the plane waiting for their arrival.

He nodded as they neared.

"Good afternoon, sirs. Flight plan is logged, plane is inspected and fueled and the weather is perfect for a nice flight today."

"Thank you, Gavin. As always, we appreciate the short notice you are always able to offer us."

Josh laughed. "Nice to see you, Gavin. Let's all pray this is an uneventful day."

"Noted." Gavin nodded and waited as they each walked up the stairs to board the GHOST plane.

The inside of the plane boasted deep, rich, brown leather seats, two by two, with each set of four facing each other. A small table sat between two sets of seats so they could pull out laptops and work while enroute.

He sat in the first seat close to the window and almost groaned when Josh sat directly across from him. Yep, there was going to be no peace and quiet.

The hatch to the airplane closed and Gavin began starting engines and getting them ready for takeoff. Both he and Josh buckled their seatbelts. His mind wandered to how much trouble they were going to find once they landed. Hopefully none.

"So, you know, I'm not letting this go."

"What do you want me to say? It's not polite to kiss and tell."

Josh chuckled again. "That right there tells me a lot. So, based on the fact that she didn't exactly want to talk to you at the shower tells me she's pissed at you. So, were you sucky in the sack? Or did you jump and run?"

"Neither, asshole."

Josh laughed but thankfully let the conversation fall away. Instead, he turned to look out the window as the plane lifted off and the ground became more distant. The thrust of the plane and the incline were the parts of flying Axel hated most, so he closed his eyes and tried not to think of takeoff. On the flight back to GHOST Bridget would be onboard and maybe he'd get the chance to find out why she left before he came back.

Both he and Josh received texts at the same time from Gaige. That probably wasn't good news. Both men gazed quickly at each other then grabbed their phones. Reading the text his heartbeat increased, his mouth became dry and he felt lightheaded. This was the worst news they could have received.

15

"Oh dear. Now you've got me scared out of my wits, Bridget."

"I know mom and I'm so sorry. But, Sophie insists that we fly down there so we are safe and they're sending a plane. Normally I would have flat out refused, but if anything happened to Aidyn, it would just kill me. Also, if anything happened to you, I would not be able to live with the guilt of it, so I hope you'll do me this favor and come along willingly. Since I'm not sure how long we'll be there, just pack the clothes you have here, we can buy more if need be. If you could pack a bag for Aidyn, I'd appreciate it. I'm going to run down to the range and grab my second range bag and my laptop. That way I can contact all of my clients and cancel classes as long as I need to."

"Honey, maybe you should wait until they get here."

"It's broad daylight right now and I'll only be gone for a few minutes. My range bag is packed, my laptop is right next to it on the desk. In and out."

Her mom was still a nice-looking woman. Bridget got her green eyes from her. She also got her nose and her smile from her. She inherited her short stature from her mom, too. Both of them were only 5' tall and she'd always wished she were taller. She's also always hated her red hair. Ginger. Copper. Red. Oh, how she'd hated those nicknames in school. The freckles on her face were a torment also. Thankfully, they'd faded some as she'd gotten older.

She stood from the table as her mom did. Stepping into her mom's outstretched arms she closed her eyes and wrapped her arms around her mom's waist. Mom hugs were the best hugs ever.

Stepping back, she smiled at her mom. "I'll be back in just a few minutes. You and Aidyn get packed and I'll pack as soon as I get back."

"Okay."

The worry in her mom's eyes felt like a hot poker in her stomach. She hated worrying her or even being the cause of them being in danger. But for the life of her, she had no idea why she was on anyone's radar anyway. She'd never seen the woman in the airport before and hadn't seen her since she'd landed, and Cobra had brought her home. It was all so weird. But, she also couldn't stop thinking it had something to do with Yvette's friend who had gone missing. And then Sophie had told her that Skye's friend and Megan's friend had also gone missing. So, someone was targeting women who knew women whose husbands worked for Gaige. But, why them and not the women in GHOST? Not that she wanted them in danger, but why peripheral women?

Shaking the morose thoughts from her head she walked to the garage door and looked back at her mom.

"Make sure the alarm is set when I leave."

"I will."

Nodding at her mom, she stepped into the garage and jumped in her vehicle. Tapping the garage door opener, she waited until it was high enough to pass under, then pulled out of the garage. Stopping once she'd cleared the door, she tapped the button again and waited for the door to close all the way. Easing out of the driveway and onto Mile Road, she thought she wanted to make sure she contacted those clients coming to the range this afternoon first. Then she'd start contacting tomorrow's clients. Then, she'd take it a day at a time, always trying to give her clients at least 24 hours' notice. All the money she was losing by doing this was certainly going to put a dent in her finances, but she'd make do. Luckily the range was paid for.

Turning off Mile Road and onto the County PP that led to the gun range, she scanned the area and saw nothing out of the ordinary. There were only a few farms on this road and the usual traffic with the occasional tractor. Once in a while there was a four-wheeler that the farm kids played around with after chores were done.

Turning into the lot of her range, she smiled and sighed when the parking lot was empty. Pulling up to the back-door, she looked around to make sure no one was around.

She shook her head and told herself to stop being so paranoid.

Jumping from her vehicle, she had her keys ready, quickly walked to the backdoor and stepped inside. Closing it and locking it behind her, she disarmed the alarm, walked to her office, just a few steps from the backdoor, and flipped the lights on. She hurried to her desk, pulled her laptop case from under it, and slid her laptop inside as well as the cord and mouse. Zipping it up, she remembered to bring her paper file with all the phone numbers of the new clients. She hadn't had time to enter their names into the computer, something she could likely do while on the plane. Tucking the file into the front of her laptop bag, she tossed it over her right shoulder, then took the strap of her range bag and pulled it up onto her left shoulder.

Feeling as though she had all she needed, she walked to the backdoor, turned off the lights and quickly exited the building, turning the key in the lock and walking to her vehicle in record time.

Opening the backdoor, she dropped her range bag on the floor behind the driver's seat, then lay her laptop on the backseat. Turning to get into the driver's seat, something sharp and hot hit her in the side of the neck. Turning her head, a man she'd never seen before stepped in front of her with a sinister look on his face. He didn't say anything. Soon, too soon, her body went limp and her eyes closed.

16

The plane had barely touched down when Axel unbuckled his seatbelt and moved to stand.

"You won't be able to get off until we stop, and the door opens for us. May as well sit. There's nothing we can do until we get there."

His heart hammered in his chest; his mood was black as the night. To say he was on edge was the understatement of the century.

Josh leaned forward and lay his arms on the table.

"Look, let's go over this again. Bridget owns a gun range. She went down to grab her laptop and her range bag. She told her mom she'd only be a few minutes. She lives about a mile away, so it should only have taken about 15 minutes, tops. When she didn't come back in a half hour, mom tried calling her. No answer. Mom tried again, no answer. Then she called the local PD, many of whom are friends of Bridget's. They showed up on the scene and found Bridget's vehicle with her laptop on the backseat and range bag on the floor behind the driver's seat. No sign of a struggle. No Bridget."

"Yeah."

"So, when we get there, we have to check out the range. Someone was there. There have to be tire tracks, footprints, something to help us figure out what happened that there'd been no struggle. She is an expert markswoman. If she'd have had the time, she'd have pulled and shot. Mom said she was carrying. She always carried."

His breathing was choppy just listening to Josh. This was not good. He inhaled and held his breath, counting to ten, then let it out slowly.

Once he'd released the air from his lungs he said, "They snuck up on her. Surprised her. Even so, she'd have fought unless they threatened her mom or this Aidyn. Or, she could have been drugged. Chloroformed. Or bashed on the head."

"There you go. Get your head in the game. What else?"

"She'd already been inside to get the laptop and range bag, so they were likely waiting for her. It's unlikely that she'd have gotten out of her car if someone had been there when she pulled in, so they were watching from somewhere nearby. Down the road perhaps. Over a hill. Won't know until we get there and see the lay of the land."

"Right."

The plane finally stopped, and Axel stood up. Josh grabbed the go bag and handed Axel his comm unit.

"Here are your earpieces. Once we get there, we'll want to waste no time."

Axel took the wireless earpieces. The hatch opened and he thought he'd just about leap out of his skin. He made it to the front of the plane in two strides surprising Gavin at the front of the plane.

"I'll be in touch as to how long we'll be here, Gavin. Thank you."

He raced past Gavin and could feel Josh on his heels as they quickly walked to the rental SUV Gaige had waiting for them.

A man stood alongside the vehicle, nodded at them as they approached and held his hand out with keys in them.

"Good afternoon, sir. I have the keys..."

Axel nabbed the keys quickly and nodded. "Thank you so much. In a hurry."

The man stepped aside, bewilderment on his face. Axel climbed in the driver's seat, Josh jumped in the passenger seat and called Gaige on the comm unit.

"We've landed and are enroute."

"Okay. I'm on this end and so is Ford."

"Roger."

Axel did his comm check. "Testing."

"Got it. Don't go in hot."

He hated being chastised but he needed to hear that.

"Roger. Not hot."

Exiting the road in front of the hangar, Josh pulled up his phone and turned the GPS on to get them to Bridget's range. He followed the directions, it was gratefully only a ten-mile trek, so they'd be there in no time. But even ten minutes felt like an eternity.

"So, I know you don't want to talk about this, but you spent one night with her, like what five-ish years ago. But yet you're acting like you've been with her this whole time. So, what gives?"

Rotating his head on his shoulders, Axel prayed the stiffness would subside. No luck.

"I don't know what to say. I've been asking myself that same question since I saw her at the shower. There was something about her. Something new. A look or a feeling, I don't fucking know. It pisses me off as much as it surprises me."

To his credit, Josh nodded and turned to watch the scenery go by. Under better circumstances he'd say this part of the state was beautiful. Lush and green and the farms they passed seemed profitable and kept in decent shape. So, it didn't seem to be an area that had fallen on hard times. More likely this was an area where three missing women would scare the shit out of every person miles around. That was good, maybe someone saw something, and they can find some leads.

Turning down County PP, Axel again looked around the area, though this time with the operative's mind. The road was curvy, the grasses along the road a bit longer. Lush farm fields with corn, full grown this time of year would easily hide a car or a human. As they came upon the driveway for the range, he smiled when he saw the name of the range, Armed and Dangerous.

Slowly pulling into the lot, he saw two black and whites and four cops milling about gathering evidence. Putting the vehicle in park, he looked over at Josh who nodded then tapped his comm unit.

"Gaige, local PD here. Are we going to have an issue?"

"You shouldn't. I called their chief earlier and he said they'd welcome any assistance we could offer. If you do, give me a call. I'll see who I can talk to and get you some clearance."

"Roger."

Exiting their SUV, they walked to the perimeter of the police tape and waited as one of the officers approached.

"This area is secured for an investigation."

"Yes, sir. We're Axel Dunbar and Josh Masters. Our boss, Gaige Vickers called your Chief earlier to get us clearance."

The young cop, likely around twenty-nine years old, name badge said "Anders", pulled his phone from his pocket and tapped twice.

"Chief, this is Anders. I have two guys here say Gaige Vickers called you and got them clearance."

Axel tried not to fidget, but he wanted to inspect the area and his patience, little that he had, was threadbare at the moment.

"Thank you, Chief."

"Chief says go on in. We're sharing information here, so anything you find we need to know, and we'll share our information with you in return."

Axel nodded and ducked easily under the police tape. Walking toward the lone vehicle in the parking lot, his heart beat wildly in his chest. His eyes scanned the area around the SUV looking for anything out of place. Anything laying on the pavement that hadn't been picked up. The driver's door was open, but nothing seemed disturbed.

A female officer, who stood next to the vehicle and was dusting it for prints moved to walk back to her kit. The shadow her body created moved away and something glinted under the vehicle.

Axel lay down next to the pavement and saw something shiny under the car. Looking back up at the officer he asked, "Do you have another pair of gloves in your kit?"

"Yes, sir." She turned and pulled two pair of gloves from her kit, handing them to Axel and Josh.

Pushing his right hand into a glove, he reached under the vehicle and pulled the object out. Bringing it into the sunlight, he looked at it closely, then looked up at Josh. "You thinking, what I'm thinking?"

17

Her mouth was as dry as cotton. She moved her tongue around in her mouth in an attempt to wet her teeth and get her saliva working. It seemed just that much effort was tiring. A feeling of floating washed over her; a sense of slight rocking back and forth threatened to lull her back to sleep. Oh, it would be so easy to let sleep overtake her again. Clearly she needed more sleep, or she wouldn't be so damned tired. Hopefully, Aidyn would sleep for a while longer.

Aidyn? The soft sounds of crying reached her ears. It sounded more like whimpering but muffled.

"Shh, be quiet or they'll come back here again." Someone whispered. A woman's voice. Not Aidyn's sweet little voice.

Trying to open her eyes, which felt heavy as if they were full of sand , she concentrated on lifting her lids. It was dark, and blurry. Nothing came into focus.

"Bridget?" the woman's voice whispered to her. Her voice was familiar.

Softly the voice once again addressed her in a whispered tone.

"Bridget, please wake up, but don't make any noise."

Her brows pinched together, her mouth began to moisten, and her eyes started to focus somewhat. Training her eyes on the wall before her, it took her a moment to realize the small square across from her was a window with a black covering over it. Slowly she tried to sit up which was more of an exertion than it should be. Making it to a sitting position, she pushed herself back to lean against a wall she felt behind her. Reaching up with her right hand to rub her eyes, the rope around her wrist sent a jolt of pain through her body. Glancing down at the rope, she saw blood smeared on her skin and her heart raced and her spine tingled with fear.

Looking in the direction of the woman who spoke to her, she saw Sydney and Jennie Lee. Both women were dirty, tied up just as she was, and it appeared as though Sydney had a badly bruised face.

Jennie Lee spoke softly to her, "They took us as we left the bar last night. We stopped for one drink after class. There was a guy hanging out by the bar watching us. We were both creeped out by him, so we decided to leave. As we approached our cars, it must have been two men who jumped out from behind us and stuck needles in our necks. Next thing we knew we were in a van tied up and blindfolded. We must not have been given as much of whatever drug was in the needles as you were. We were taken to this place on the outskirts of town, as best we can tell."

Raising her left hand, she felt where the side of her neck stung and slowly she remembered starting to leave her range, a sharp pain in her neck and a man to the side of her moved in front of her, and then everything went dark.

Her eyes shifted to Sydney's. She'd been crying and she had a large dark spot on her cheek, where she'd likely been hit.

"What happened to you, Sydney?"

"I fought one of them when I tried to escape. Tried to run. Scratched him. He punched me in the face and rang my bell good. I've had a pounding headache since." Sydney sniffed. "Then he was chastised by one of the others for hitting me. Something that sounded like merchandise."

Bridget swallowed. "What do they sound like?"

"Ukrainian, most likely, I'd say based on the accents of my grandparent's generation," Jennie Lee responded. "They mostly whisper. There were other women in this cabin or shack. They took some of them out early this morning. I heard something about a flight somewhere."

She'd heard about sex trafficking rings. This certainly sounded like that. She swallowed the bile that threatened to rise further in her throat. Now more than ever she needed to keep her wits about her and not crack under the pressure. Thoughts of Aidyn and her mom ran through her head and she blinked rapidly to stave off the tears. Her mom would be so worried.

Jennie Lee then whispered. "I heard them say something about those ghost bastards paying for this. I don't know what that means."

"Did you hear anything else about them? Maybe we can figure out who they mean."

Sydney spat out. "Why should we care about anyone else? They're going to sell us off to be fucking sex slaves."

Bridget inhaled deeply and let her breath out slowly, she needed to think that there was a way out, a way to escape. And, if there was one small chance of it, she was damned sure going to take it. Now that her mind was clearing, and her thoughts were turning to survival, she remembered Sophie was sending someone to come and escort her and her family to Lynyrd Station to keep them safe. That thought raised two others. First, they'd reached her mom and Aidyn and taken them away. Second, maybe Gaige's team was ghost. Since she knew that Yvette had a friend go missing and so did Skye and Megan, it seemed likely that was why she was targeted, a friend of Sophie's. So, they were targeting women who had anything to do with Gaige's group.

Then, Axel's face flashed before her eyes. Axel was part of that group. And, though no one knew it except Sophie, Axel was Aidyn's father. Closing her eyes, she sent up a silent prayer that the connection wouldn't be made, and Aidyn wouldn't pay for being Axel's son.

"Whatever we have to do, we're getting out of here."

Jennie Lee's voice held some hope when she responded. "Now you're talking. Let's figure this bullshit out and go home."

Bridget nodded. "That sounds like a plan. You need to tell me anything else you may have heard. How many other women have you seen and were they all drugged like we were? Were they kept in here with you or somewhere else? Did they keep them drugged? Do you have any idea what type of drug they're using? How many men are there? Tell me everything."

Sydney straightened up and angrily swiped at the tears in her eyes.

"There were three of them that I saw. When I tried escaping, I ran into another room in the cabin. I was disoriented and thought it was the front door. But, it was another room; there was no furniture in it. But there were four women in it. Each of them chained to a wall, the middle of the wall so they couldn't touch each other or help each other out. Two of them looked drugged, their heads were bent down, and they were leaning over. Two of them were awake it seemed. One of them looked frightened when I burst through the door and she shrieked. The other one just stared at me, almost hopeful. But then one of the men grabbed me by the hair and dragged me out of the room and that's when he hit me."

"Do you know if all four of the women were removed from the shack today?"

Jennie Lee then answered. "I think they only took two of them because one of the men was left behind. The only reason for that would be to guard the women."

"Could be. Are there two of them driving this van?"

18

The shiny object he held in his hand was a broken needle. It looked like it had been dropped and it broke. There was a small amount of substance dripping from it, but hopefully enough to know what drug was used.

Josh looked at the small object and his jaw tightened.

"So, they're sneaking up on the women and drugging them. That takes the fight out of them and the bastards can whisk them away without a scene being made."

"That's my guess." His jaw tightened as well. This whole thing has been too personal. Too targeted and too smarmy. Plus, by not aiming at the teams' women but rather females the GHOST women knew, it was impossible to predict who'd they select next. There was no way they could protect everyone associated with their wives.

Axel's brows scrunched together. "Also, the fact that in the past, when Yvette's ex, Caulfield took women to sell, he took much younger women. Now they're targeting women in their thirties and forties. Another change in pattern. We have to find out who Caulfield was selling to and whether who's running the operation has added any sellers who prefer older women. Right now, we have to go check on Bridget's mom and this Aidyn fella."

Josh pulled his phone from his pocket. "Sophie sent me Bridget's address. Her mom is there. It's only about a mile from here."

"Let's go." Carefully handing his evidence to the police officer, he said, "You'll make sure we're notified when you have identified the substance being used?"

"Yes, sir." She pulled a small notebook from her pocket. "Gaige Vickers has given a command about all contact information and from what my Chief tells me, he'll be contacting our office often to make sure he knows what's happening."

Axel nodded. "Thank you."

"Yes, sir. Thank you for what you are doing. I admire it."

Axel paused. Usually, Gaige wouldn't offer up much information about what they did for a living, but he must have had to make an exception to ensure information probably because of the women who'd been taken.

Nodding at the officer he started walking to the rental. Stopping quickly, he turned to the officer once again. "Thank you for what you are doing. We all need each other."

The officer smiled and for the first time he thought she was an attractive woman, even in her uniform.

Jumping into the rental he and Josh headed out of the lot as Josh gave him the directions from his phone.

"Turn right up ahead onto Mile Road."

Glancing all around for anything that looked out of place he tried to stem the rising frustration surrounding Bridget's capture and the fact that he was about to meet Aidyn. Both of these situations were awkward. The last thing he wanted to do was to protect the boyfriend or husband of a woman he'd slept with and still thought about. His jaw clenched and his teeth ground.

"You keep grinding your teeth and clenching your jaw you're going to have all kinds of trouble. What's with you lately?"

"Nothing."

"Doesn't seem like nothing. As a matter of fact, it seems like something. So, other than the fact that you and Bridget slept together about five years ago, was there more?"

"No."

"Hmm..." Josh turned to look at his phone again. "The next house on the left."

He slowed down then pulled into the driveway. It was a nice little house. A small ranch-style house with a two-car garage. The white siding and the burgundy trim and shutters contrasted with the green trees and fields surrounding it. The blacktop driveway was freshly done and the deep black leading up to the white house impressed Axel. Neat. Tidy. Nice.

There were no cars in the driveway and the shades had been pulled.

He swallowed. Back where he came from the only time you closed all the shades during the day was when the family was in mourning. I suppose they were in a sense. But he'd do whatever he could to find her. There'd be no stopping him.

Inhaling to fill his lungs he unbuckled his seatbelt and stepped out of the rental vehicle. Josh was about two steps ahead of him. Walking to the front door his stomach twisted but he concentrated on keeping his breathing even and steady.

Josh knocked on the door and a voice sounded from a microphone.

"Who is there?"

Axel looked up and saw the camera trained on them. "Axel Dunbar and Josh Masters. We were sent here by Sophie Vickers."

"Okay. Do you have ID?"

Both he and Josh pulled out their badges, which looked official like law enforcement ones, but actually were only gold badges that said "Special Operative" in case they needed them, much like now.

The turning locks on the other side of the door had him turning to face the door. Josh stood in front of him, but he easily peered over Josh's shoulder.

The door opened, only an inch at first, Josh held his badge up for a closer look and the woman behind the door seemed satisfied enough to open it all the way.

"I'm sorry. I'm so shaken up by..." She turned and looked behind her, then back to them. Her voice softened when she finished her sentence. "By Bridget's disappearance."

Her eyes teared up and she took a deep breath. Opening the screen door still between them, she smiled weakly and said, "Please, come in."

She stepped back allowing them entrance and he looked around at the house. It seemed so much like Bridget. Everything was neat and tidy; the furniture was no nonsense brown leather furniture in good shape and clean. No frilly floral sofa or chairs or curtains. Everything went together but was a sensible color and style.

When his eyes turned back to the woman, he was disconcerted to see her staring at him, her brows bunched together.

He held his right hand out to formally introduce himself. "Axel Dunbar."

She stared at him so long he felt uncomfortable. He raised his left eyebrow, something he often did when inquiring or questioning and she quickly shook her head as if shaking her thoughts away and took his hand in a firm handshake.

"Vivian Barnes."

Josh then held his hand out. "Josh Masters."

Vivian shook his hand, too, then looked at Axel once again.

"Grandma is that Momma?"

19

The van turned a sharp corner and Bridget hit her head on the side wall. The road became terribly bumpy and the women found themselves tossed around. The rope bit into her right wrist and when they were bumped and thrown around the searing pain jolted up her arm. Trying to be quiet so the men in the front didn't hear them talking, she tried not crying out but instead grunted under her breath and vowed even harder to escape.

Reaching up with her left hand to try and untie the rope that held her to a hook in the side of one of the reinforcement walls on the van. She struggled and dug with her fingernails to loosen the rope but had no luck. The van came to a stop and she quickly looked over at Jennie Lee and Sydney.

Taking a deep breath when she saw Sydney close her eyes, Bridget prepared herself for what would come next. Whatever that was.

"Listen. Pay attention to everything without looking like you are. Anything you can notice. Sounds. Smells. Everything."

Jennie Lee responded. "Okay."

Sydney nodded but said nothing. She looked like she was about to cry again, so likely saying anything would begin the waterworks, and now more than ever, she needed to be able to pay attention.

The sounds of the doors closing caused her breath to hitch and she took another deep breath and let it out slowly.

The backdoors opened and two men wearing masks jumped into the van, one of them walked to her and grabbed the rope that held her roughly and pulled a large knife from his back, then sliced the rope from the van, leaving the part tied to her intact. The dried blood on her wrist opened when he jerked her arm to pull her from the van, but she ground her teeth together and didn't say a word or cry out. She decided to play the meek captive to keep from getting her lights punched out so she could pay attention and plan.

She heard Sydney softly crying behind her and hoped she could pull herself together to help them figure things out.

Bridget was jerked from the van by her arm and hair then roughly dragged along to inside a cabin. Two steps up into the porch on the cabin and what looked like an area littered with garbage and dirty buckets held yard working implements.

It was a couple steps through this room and through another door to enter the cabin. It wasn't as filthy as the porch area and for some odd reason she was grateful for that. She was roughly pushed onto a vinyl kitchen chair. There was a table sitting a few inches from her. Her left arm was pulled behind the chair and tied to the back of the chair with another rough rope which now bit into her left wrist. Jennie Lee was brought in next and treated much the same way. Her longer, brown hair had become disheveled and the ponytail she'd worn yesterday was askew but not completely undone. Some of her hair hung over her face and she kept her eyes averted to the table. Likely best they didn't look at each other.

The two men said something to each other in Ukrainian, something she recognized from her Army days. But she didn't understand the words, just the dialect. One then left while the other started rummaging in a cooler on the floor to her right.

Turning, he started tossing meal bars on the table along with bottles of water. So, this was to be their meals. It was a good sign that they were being fed but that also likely meant they were to be kept healthy to sell, that thought hit her hard in the stomach. She'd likely end up dead because there was no fucking way she was going to live as a sex slave the rest of her life. But she'd do her best to get away and maybe that meant die trying.

Soon Sydney was brought in and seated in another chair, tied and shoved to the table. In a strong accent one of the men said, "Eat."

Reaching forward with her right hand for her meal bar, her eyes landed on the dried blood and abrasions on her wrist and her anger settled itself deeply. These bastards would pay and dearly.

Picking up her meal bar, she brought it to her mouth and ripped the package with her teeth, then began eating the cardboard tasting food. She'd need to keep her strength up, so she'd eat. Sydney didn't reach for her bar and the order came out stronger this time.

"Eat. Now."

Sydney sniffled and Bridget didn't want her to get beaten or killed so she looked at Sydney and repeated their order.

"Eat your food."

Sydney looked at her, a tear slid down her cheek, but she slowly reached for the bar and ripped the package with her teeth and began eating. A quick glance at Jennie Lee to see that she was eating, and Bridget took another bite of her meal bar and tried getting it down. Reaching for the water bottle, she struggled to open it with one hand only to hear the Ukrainian shit heads laughing. Bringing the water bottle to her mouth, she bit down on the cap and twisted the bottle opening it.

They stopped laughing and started speaking in their language, which Bridget tried to understand, but nothing sounded familiar. She decided to focus on eating and any other sounds outside. She heard a boat motor or something similar and figured they were either close to water or an ATV trail or something where a smaller engine would run. She wasn't able to see much, the dusk had settled in.

Jennie Lee and Sydney both followed her lead to open their water bottles and the women sat in silence eating their meager meals and drinking their water. The sounds of another vehicle approaching the cabin sent the man outside.

The only thing she could figure was they were bringing the other women to the cabin. She heard a scream from outside and a gunshot, and her meal bar threatened to explode from her stomach.

20

V ivian turned to the little boy who came from the other room.

She turned to him. "Oh, honey, no. I'm sorry but not yet."

"Oh." His head bowed down in sadness.

Vivian knelt and pulled the little boy into her arms.

"It's okay, Aidyn, these men are going to take us to stay in a safe place until we can find Momma."

Aidyn? Aidyn? Her son? She had a son?

"But Gram, Momma won't know where to find us."

"Yes, she will. She asked these men to come and get us. She'll know how to find us."

Aidyn's head looked up and his eyes landed on Axel's. Mesmerized by those hazel eyes and that brown hair Axel stared in amazement at him. It was like looking at a miniature version of himself. Except he wasn't.

He nodded at Aidyn. "That's true. She'll know to come to our home to find you. And you and your grandma will be very safe there."

"Let's go and get your suitcase so we can leave." Vivian ushered Aidyn into another room. She looked back at them and said, "We'll only be a minute, we're all packed."

Then they disappeared down a hallway. He stood staring long after they'd disappeared, then Josh finally broke his silence.

"You didn't tell me you had a son."

He jerked as if he'd been hit then looked at Josh. "I don't."

"You're kidding me, right? That kid looks just like you."

"She..." He swallowed because frankly he didn't know what to say. His heart raced in his chest. It pounded so hard he felt like he was going to throw up. "She never told me anything about a baby."

His feelings changed so quickly from disbelief to anger then back to disbelief to anger he felt like a teenage girl.

Vivian and Aidyn came back with suitcases and Aidyn was wearing a cute little Pokémon backpack. He looked at the boy, really looked at him. Same eyes. Same hair. Except Axel's was now longer. Same nose.

"How old are you, Aidyn?"

Aidyn looked at his fingers and held four up proudly. "Four. And some more."

Vivian laughed. "He's about four and a half."

She patted Aidyn on the head and Axel's world spun around before him. About four and a half. He'd been with Bridget a little over five years ago. The timing was uncanny.

Josh broke the awkward silence. "Okay, Vivian do you have everything turned off that needs to be off? We can get going, we have a private plane waiting."

"Yes, we're all set."

As they exited the front of the house Axel's phone rang. He answered as his eyes watched as Aidyn walked to the SUV and Vivian helped him climb in. She reached in and buckled his seatbelt then climbed in next to him in the back.

"Dunbar."

Gaige started talking without announcing himself. "They are using Ketamine. It renders them unconscious for a while until they can get them tied and transported."

"Is this something easy to get? Do you have to have a prescription for it?"

"Yes, it's prescribed. We're now searching for records of large doses of Ketamine being purchased in Indianapolis. We'll branch out from there."

"Thanks. Keep me posted. And, is Sophie close to you? I need to ask her a question."

Gaige was silent for a time and he wondered if he'd already hung up.

The phone sounded like it bobbled a bit and finally after a long silence he heard Sophie's voice.

"Hey Axel, have you found Bridget yet?"

"No. Is Aidyn my son?"

"What makes you ask such a question?"

"Don't fucking jerk me around. Is he my son?"

He felt bad snapping at her, but it just pissed him off with her coy bullshit.

Sophie sighed. "Yes. She told me this morning. She said if anything happened to her that I should tell you."

"Something did happen to her."

"Yes. But we're going to find her, and she'll be back with Aidyn. I have to believe that. You all are amazing at what you do. We just have to find her alive and well."

He heard her voice hitch and knew she was emotional. Pregnant and her friend laid a heavy secret on her and then disappeared.

"Look Soph, I'm sorry. I didn't mean to ..."

"It's okay. When Bridget said if something happens to me, I took it as if she died so you'd be able to raise Aidyn. And, honestly I had hoped she'd be the one to tell you."

"Yeah. Put Gaige back on please."

He heard Sophie tell Gaige to take the phone and his heartbeat quickened.

"Yeah."

"I'm not sure what to do now. He's mine. I want to protect him. But, I also need to find Bridget."

"You and Josh need to stay there and find Bridget. Put Vivian and Aidyn on the plane. Gavin will get them back here. We'll watch over them until you bring Bridget back here."

He scraped his hand down the side of his face while staring at his son in the back of a rental vehicle. What a day already.

"You, roger?"

"Roger. On our way to the airport now."

"I'll call Gavin and have him at the ready."

The call ended and his feet refused to move. He'd always wanted to be a father. He'd wanted kids when he had no business wanting kids. But, he wanted the whole ball of wax, the wife, the house, the dog, the kids. He'd left that dream behind years ago thinking his chance was over. Now here he is with a son he'd never met. No wife. No house. No dog. Instead, his son's mother is missing, and he has to try and find her. He has to let his son go to a house where no one knows him, and he knows no one else. Except his grandmother. She's with him. This was the absolute right thing to do. It was also the most difficult. He wanted to stay with Aidyn.

Josh caught his attention with a hands up as in what the hell gesture and he made his feet move him forward. Climbing in the rental, he buckled his seatbelt turned the key in the ignition and backed out of the driveway. Glancing in the rearview mirror he looked at his son. His sweet face, trying so hard to be brave, clutching a stuffed toy he'd brought with him. His heart was close to exploding.

Josh nudged him. "You want me to drive?"

Shaking his head, he put his thoughts right. "No."

The car ride to the airport was mostly silent. Not many questions asked. He was grateful to have the time to get his thoughts in order. Pulling up to the private plane, Aidyn's eyes got big.

"Wow. Are we going in that?"

Vivian answered, "Yes, we are sweety."

"I've never been in a plane before."

"No, you haven't. How fun!"

Stopping the vehicle, he climbed out and opened the backdoor. He helped Aidyn unbuckle his seatbelt. Then lifted him down from the SUV. Holding his little hand, he walked him to the plane and introduced him to Gavin.

Gavin leaned down and shook Aidyn's hand like a grown man then said, "I'll make sure you have a smooth flight and get you to Lynyrd Station within the hour."

"Thank you." Aidyn said.

Axel walked him up the steps to the inside of the plane, sat him in the same seat he'd sat in on the way here and buckled him in. Vivian sat across from him.

Axel then sat in the empty seat next to Aidyn and said, "Josh and I won't be going with you and your grandma. We're going to stay back and help find your momma. But, Sophie is your momma's friend and she's waiting for you to get to the compound and she'll make sure you and Grandma are comfortable and safe there."

Aidyn looked into his eyes and then over to his grandma. "Do you know Sophie?"

"Yes, sweetheart I do. She's very nice and she is a very good friend of your momma's."

"Okay." Aidyn scooted back in his seat and Axel's heart swelled. What a wonderful brave young man he was. Just as Axel stood to leave the plane, Aidyn turned to him.

"You promise you'll bring my Momma back?"

"I absolutely promise I'll do everything I can to find her and bring her back to you."

Aidyn thought for a moment, then nodded his satisfaction with that answer.

Axel looked over at Vivian. "Are you alright about this?"

She smiled, her head cocked to the left slightly she said, "Yes. We'll be fine. You just go find my girl."

21

One of her captors untied her hand from the back of the chair, grabbed her by the hair roughly and proceeded to half drag her, half escort her to another room in the cabin. It was a small cabin, but she managed to keep her head up while she was forced to walk through what could be called the living area, so she could see as much as possible. Noticing two closed doors, she mentally imprinted where they were. She was pushed against one door while her captor unlocked it with his free hand.

Once unlocked, she noted that he wore his keys on a ring from his belt for easy access. He twisted the knob on the door and thrust her inside where she stumbled but didn't fall. He pointed to the wall to the right of the door, which when the door was open, was partially covered.

"Sit." he barked.

She saw the metal ring screwed to the wall close to a corner and knew she'd be tied up again to sit in this miser-

able room. Hopefully she'd be allowed to use the bathroom at some point.

She sat against the wall and slightly aside from the ring on
her left side, the corner on her right and Igor, or whatever
his name was, grabbed her wrist with the rope still
attached and tied her to the ring. She refused to watch
what he was doing but she did count the times he
threaded the rope through a loop. Three. Three times
she'd need to unloop to get away.

Once he finished with his handiwork, he stood back,
nudged her leg with his foot and gruffly said, "Hey."

She looked up, still reminding herself to remain contrite
looking though anger and hatred seethed through her.
When she met his eyes, a sick smile creased his face. "You
be good. Ya?"

Nodding she then waited for him to turn away before
daring to look around the room. There was a ring on each
wall just like the one her wrist was tied to, close to the
corners. Her hand wasn't over her head, but more to her
left even with her shoulder. He didn't cut this rope like he
had in the van and there was a tail left on the rope about a
foot long. There was one window in the room, completely
boarded up so no light shone into the room except the
waning light from the living area where he left the door
open. Likely to bring in Sydney and Jennie Lee.

On the wall across from her there was a light fixture
attached to the top of the wall, and the wire ran up the
wall and was loosely attached with bent nails in about two
places.

She heard scuffling and a chair slide back and then the uneven footsteps of someone being half dragged through the room and knew it was likely Jennie Lee being brought in. Sydney would be crying.

She averted her eyes to the floor and waited until Igor and Jennie Lee were in the room. Once he had her sitting on the floor and his back was to her, she watched how he tied her rope and memorized it. The rope wasn't all that thick, but it was abrasive, likely on purpose to keep them from struggling against it. It bit into her skin with each rough movement. The sticky wetness of blood could be felt on her wrist now. More new cuts.

Igor issued the same command to Jennie Lee. "Be good."

Jennie Lee nodded, and he turned to exit but not before stopping to look at her. She kept her head and eyes averted and he must have been satisfied because he moved on to bring Sydney back.

Just as suspected, Sydney yelped when she was roughly grabbed and whimpered most of the way back to their room. Igor roughly shoved Sydney into the room and she stumbled and fell emitting a sob which only made Igor laugh. In his broken gruff English, he hissed, "Baby."

Sydney scooted across the floor to sit in the corner to her right and Jennie Lee's left. Igor grabbed her hand roughly and tied it to the ring and Bridget began counting the loops. Two, only two. If they could talk Sydney into untying herself, she could help them escape.

Igor left the room and closed the door. Bridget heard the key turn in the lock and let out a long breath. She listened to hear how soundproof the room actually was and how easily it would be to hear them talking outside. She noted that the logs in the cabin offered a fair amount of sound-proofing, but not completely. They'd still need to be careful.

Sydney broke the silence first. "Do you think they shot someone?"

Bridget looked over at her, though there was virtually no light in the room, she could see her outline and the whites of her eyes but that was about it.

"Probably shot at someone who tried to run. If we're their merchandise, they won't kill us."

"Fuckers."

That got a smile from Bridget. Sydney was beginning to get more mad than scared. Perfect.

More scuffling could be heard and uneven footsteps and they each looked down at the floor as the door was unlocked. The door opened and in stumbled another woman, shoved just like the rest of them, but she didn't fall. The light that shone in the door allowed her to see the woman had blonde hair, about shoulder length. She was wearing jeans, ankle boots and a dirty white t-shirt. Just like the rest of them, whatever they'd been wearing when they were taken is how they were dressed. Luckily she had been down at her shooting range, so she wore jeans, range boots which were similar to the boots she wore in the Army, and a dark blue t-shirt. Jennie Lee and Sydney were dressed similarly because they'd just been shooting before going out.

Igor tied up the new girl, told her to behave and left the room, locking the door behind him.

Bridget softly said, "I'm Bridget."

"Jennie Lee."

"Sydney."

"I'm Riah."

Wracking her brain, she remembered Sophie telling her about a Riah. It was an unusual name, so it stuck.

"You're Skye Montgomery's friend."

"Yes." She shifted her position. "You know Skye? Oh my God, she's not here is she?"

"Shh. No, she's not here, and yes, I've met her. I'm Sophie's friend."

"What are the odds of that happening?"

"No odds. Deliberate."

"No. Fucking. Way."

"Yeah, but we're going to get out of here."

22

Getting into the rental vehicle once again, Axel let out a heavy sigh. Right now, his focus had to be on finding Bridget. Then, once she was back at the compound, he'd ring her neck for not telling him he had a son.

Grabbing his phone first, he dialed Sophie's number. He set his phone in the drink holder between the seats and waited while Josh buckled in.

Driving away from the plane, he glanced in his rearview mirror to see the body of the plane as he drove away. One of the hardest moments in his life right now was finding a son, only to have to put his son on a plane to go away from him. All he really wanted to do was sit and watch his son play and jump and be a little boy.

"Hi, Axel." Sophie's voice broke into his thoughts.

"I just had to put Aidyn and Vivian on the GHOST plane, which is likely the hardest thing I've ever done. You need to have someone meet them at the airport and then I'm tasking you with taking care of them until I return with Bridget."

"I'll take good care of them. I've already told Jax, Skye, Yvette, Megan and Roxanne. Among all of us, if I go into labor, we'll be sure someone is with them and they are safe. They can stay in Jax's old rooms here."

"Okay. Thanks."

"Axel, it'll be alright."

"How about when you have this baby, someone comes and takes it away and you don't find out where it was for four and a half years? Would you say that was okay?"

"No. But, I didn't do that to you. And, it's the reality of your life right now. Deal with it. Being angry won't change it. Find Bridget and you two work it out. I'm trying to help."

He kept his eyes on the road but clenched his teeth together. "Got it." Jerking his head to the left he finished the call with a softer tone. "I'm sorry, Soph. Thank you."

"Roger."

The call ended and Josh spoke for the first time in a long while.

"You were pretty tough on her. Shows how tough she is that she didn't start crying. Hormones and all."

"Yeah, she's badass."

"If you aren't careful, she's going to kick your ass and the others just might enjoy watching it. Get your head on straight, man."

He turned out of the airport and onto the road leading them back to the gun range, the GHOST plane flew over them and Axel watched the best way he could as his son flew away from him.

"I've got it. Let's go find Bridget and the other women so I can go get to know my son."

"Now you're talking. First thing is Vivian gave me the keys to the house and she said Bridget kept notes in her laptop of important events. Sort of like a diary. Maybe there's information there on the woman from the airport. Also, we can stay there and use it as our base camp here."

"Gaige said the police also found Bridget's phone laying on the driver's seat. Likely who ever took her pulled it from her pocket to leave there so she wouldn't be traced. Why don't you call and see if they have anything from the phone? The last few pictures or calls."

Josh pulled his phone out and began working. Axel tried not looking up at the sky for the GHOST plane and focusing his attention on the plans they needed to make instead.

Following the roads back to Bridget's house Axel started running over the evidence they currently had. They were using Ketamine to sedate the women so there was no fight. Bridget felt followed right from Daggert Winery.

"Josh, see if you can find out which Uber driver picked Bridget up at Daggert. She felt followed from there. Maybe he or she will be able to give us some information on the vehicle or license plate. Also, the airport. Once we have the Uber driver, get the time he dropped Bridget at the airport. He'd have the time and place on his app. Then we'll need the airport security camera footage for that date and time. Let's see if we can find the vehicle that followed them and get the plate number and a visual on the woman following Bridget. There should be visuals of the woman at the airport, too."

"Shit. Now you're on fire."

He listened as Josh relayed the information to Gaige and Ford. Both of them began working immediately on their tasks. He turned into Bridget's driveway and let out a deeply held breath.

He and Josh hopped out of the vehicle, grabbed their go bags from the back and headed to the front entry. Josh tossed him the keys while he continued texting and Axel opened the door. Dropping his go bag on the floor, he looked around the room and remembered the first time he saw Aidyn. His heartbeat quickened. Walking through the living room and down the hall he'd watched Aidyn and Vivian take, he looked for his bedroom. It was easy to find, the colorful myriad of toys and games lying about, the primary blue bedspread and the red pillow were certainly a child's room colors. The white bed and matching dresser were neat. Someone had made the small twin bed this morning but left some of Aidyn's toys lying about. He likely couldn't decide which toys to take with him.

A picture on his dresser of Bridget and Aidyn, at a park, looked recent if Aidyn's age in the picture were to be believed. He picked up the picture and stared into her green eyes. Her reddish hair glowing around her beautiful face gave her the look of an angel. But the fully angelic person in the picture was Aidyn. He smiled at the camera, his adorable face so much like a younger version of himself. His son. What did Bridget think every time she looked at Aidyn?

"We've got a plate." Josh yelled from the living room. "Searching now."

Axel pulled himself from his thoughts and walked across the hall to Bridget's room. It was clear based on the pictures of Aidyn in this room that this was hers. He swallowed a huge lump in his throat and looked around at the family pictures of them together. Without him.

Jerking his head to change the direction of his thoughts he noticed her laptop on the desk. The police department had her work laptop, but they didn't have this one. He proceeded to open it and then played around a few times to see if he could come up with a password. Aidyn. Aidyn1. Family. Nothing. Going to the living room he grabbed his go bag and pulled out their little password scanner and plugged it into Bridget's laptop.

Turning it on, he watched as it ran a myriad of passwords through her laptop to get into her computer. Walking away for a few moments, he opened her closet and let out a breath. No male clothing in here, she lived with Aidyn and no one else. Except maybe her mom. He'd yet to find her room.

Touching a couple of her blouses he searched through the closet looking for anything else that might be a clue. Moving the clothing away from the back of the closet his heartbeat damned near stopped as he stared at something he never believed he'd see.

23

Bridget shifted her weight so she could kneel. It rose her up enough that she could feel the bracket that held the metal ring fastened to the wall at about her shoulder height. Running the fingers of her right hand over the bracket, she felt for any sharp or rough edges. Anything that could be used to cut through the ropes.

Finding the edge of one of the screws she proceeded to run the rope over the edge of the screw feeling quite satisfied when she heard rope tearing.

"Are you cutting your rope on something?" Jennie Lee whispered.

"Yes. One of the screws holding the ring is rough enough that I can cut through small bits at a time."

She heard Jennie Lee and one of the other women shift their weight and begin looking for rough patches to begin sawing through their ropes. The room next to them was beginning to fill up with more women, which diverted their captors' attention from this room for the time being. Even though the pulling and tugging on the rope bit into her left wrist, Bridget wasn't stopping. Nothing could keep her from breaking free if she still had a breath in her body.

Soon enough the rope began to fray in earnest and though her body was warm from the exertion she continued until finally she felt the rope give way. A final tug and she was free. From the wall at least. The biggest hurdle was yet to come.

She whispered to the others in the room. "I'm free."

"Me, too." Jennie Lee whispered.

Bridget sat against the wall for a moment to plan out her next move. Their next move.

"We have to be careful. What we know for sure is there are two of them out there, now likely three of them because of the vehicle that brought Riah and others. Keep your hand with the rope on it close to the ring in case they walk in. We need to look as though we are restrained until we know what we should do next."

Jennie Lee asked, "Riah, what happened out there with the gunshot?"

"One of the girls kicked one of those assholes in the knee and he fell to the ground then pulled his weapon and shot in the direction she ran."

"Did he kill her?"

"I don't know. I was dragged in here."

Bridget then asked. "Do they all have guns?"

"From what I could tell, yes."

Okay, that wasn't an issue if she could get her hands on one of the guns. The same was true of Jennie Lee. She wasn't so sure about Sydney, right now. Jennie Lee and Sydney, if she snapped out of it, could shoot if they had the guns. As for herself, she knew so much about guns, she could shoot damned near anything. She just needed the opportunity to grab one of the guns.

Sydney finally said, "I'm free."

She then stood and began feeling around the window above her head. Slowly, she found a loose piece of the wood and quietly pulled it back far enough to see outside. They were at the back of the cabin instead of the driveway side which was good and bad. It was good that they could pry the wood off the window, but bad that they couldn't see how many vehicles were in the driveway.

One of the women from the room next door started shouting and kicking the wall. They all froze to listen to what happened. They could hear the door being unlocked and then a loud smack and a body thud against the wall. Bridget swallowed the anger and bile that rose from her stomach. These fuckers would pay. Momentarily, Bridget wondered about the women in the next room. Had any other friends of the wives been kidnapped, too? Shaking off the thought, she came back to their predicament.

Bridget then had a plan. "Okay. I'm going to scream and get that son of a bitch in here. Once he's in the room one of you needs to quietly close the door because we can't be sure no one has come back.

Riah said, "I'll close the door."

"When he comes at me to hit me, I'm going to kick him and blow out his knee. If it doesn't work, I'll need all of you to jump on his back to give me time to grab his weapon."

Sydney spoke up first, "No, I'll scream. You need to be ready to grab his weapon, I noticed that he kidney carries."

"Are you sure, Syd?"

"Yes. You're much better with weapons and surer of yourself. Just get it right, we only have one shot at this."

Without any more discussion, Sydney began screaming and Jennie Lee joined in. The key in the door could be heard and Igor or whoever walked into the room. Riah, jumped in front of the door and closed it while Igor stomped across the room to silence Sydney. Bridget wasted no time. Sucking in a deep breath she quickly walked the few steps across the room before Igor could react to the door closing and she grabbed his weapon. He twisted quickly and her hand slipped off the gun. Sydney then jumped up and ripped parts of the board on the window off allowing a bit of light to seep into the room. It allowed Jennie Lee to see that Bridget needed help and she kicked Igor in the nuts. Hard. So hard he fell instantly to the floor with Bridget on his back. She righted herself and grabbed his weapon.

"Any rope length to tie this fucker up?"

Riah responded, "Not enough to tie him up."

Bridget looked down at him and slammed him hard in the head with the butt of the pistol. He stilled which gave them just a moment before the other captor opened the door. As he stepped in, he saw Igor laying on the ground and pulled his weapon, but Bridget had him first, two shots and he fell to the ground. She grabbed his weapon and handed it to Jennie Lee.

"Once we make sure there are no others here, one of you get our captors' keys and knives and cut the others out of that room. I'm going out to see if there is a vehicle for us to get the hell out of here."

Bridget slowly rounded the door knowing full well if there was anyone else here, they would have run in by now. But, you could never be too cautious.

Stepping from the room with Jennie Lee behind her, Sydney and Riah grabbed knives from their captors' belts as well as their keys and worked on unlocking the other door. As they walked through the kitchen area, there was a box of meal bars on the counter and Bridget grabbed a couple for herself and tucked them in her pocket. Not sure what would come next, survival came first.

She quietly stepped through the kitchen door and out to the screened porch and crouched down. Peering outside she only saw a four-wheeler sitting off to the side of the driveway.

"You want to go for help, or do you want me to go?" she asked Jennie Lee.

"You go. I'll stay here and round up whatever ammo I can find, any weapons and food. We'll leave the cabin, so we aren't sitting ducks in case those fuckers come back. But we'll be just inside the woods over there."

She pointed to an area.

Bridget looked at her and smiled. "Okay. Keep making your way down the driveway but stay hidden and stay together. I'm going down the driveway to make time. I'll stop at the first house I see to call for help."

Bridget stepped inside quickly to see if there was any ammo and found a box on the sofa table. She grabbed a handful of bullets, pocketed them, then went back out the door. Jennie Lee still stood watching for any movement.

"All clear so far."

24

A picture that she'd taken of the two of them, laying side by side in bed after they'd had sex the second time that evening. She'd said it was because looking at a picture of two people together was the truest way to see if they belonged together. Body language, even if the whole body doesn't show, is a factor for compatibility. She took the picture with her phone then they looked at it together.

Both of them were smiling, their eyes were relaxed, their facial expressions happy and together they looked...fantastic. Her green eyes and his hazel-colored eyes were stunning together. He remembered it even back then. Their hair color, hers reddish brown, his brown or dark blond she'd said. The two colors lying next to each other complimented the other. Their skin tones, while his skin was tanned and weathered more than hers, she had a healthy glow that radiated beauty, fit together perfectly. That was just it, she was radiant. And, very likely at that moment pregnant with Aidyn.

He inhaled deeply and slowly let his breath release from his lungs. What had she said to him? "You told me your name was Robert Beckman." Fuuuck. She didn't know his name.

Tucking the picture back on the shelf it sat on, he turned and left the closet. Looking at the laptop he saw that his password scrambler did its job and he was now able to access her laptop.

The first thing he did was click on the Photo's icon and started looking through her photos. His eyes landed on Aidyn as a baby. Bridget holding him and kissing his little head. She snuggled with him often and these pictures showed it. They laughed a lot. There were hundreds of pictures of them doing things together. Then, a picture taken just last week was a selfie, of them laying side by side on the floor of this room by the looks of the rug, both smiling, heads together. Just like the picture in her closet.

Tears sprung to his eyes and he sniffed and then cleared his throat. He had to stay strong. He had to find her.

Finding the folder dated the day of the shower he saw the pictures of Bridget and Sophie together, some of the shower decorations and the last one was of a dark-haired woman on a plane. There was a look of surprise on her face as Bridget snapped the photo. Looking through her messages he saw that Bridget had forwarded it to a Cobra. Scrolling back on their messages it seemed that she'd asked him to come to the airport because she was scared about the woman following her. He should have been the one to protect her.

"We've got something." Josh said from the doorway.

"We've got the plates on the vehicle. Gaige and Ford have been scouring records along with everyone else available and they found the plates registered to Fedir Bulikov. Turns out Fedir has a hunting shack just about 30 minutes from here. Coincidentally, it was purchased just four months ago."

"Hmm, they wouldn't have known about Bridget that long ago, but they likely had plans to begin scouring this area for women in the coming months. I understand they move their sex trafficking operations around to avoid capture. Let's go find them."

He didn't need a renewed sense of purpose for finding her. But they did need this lead and he started feeling more hopeful than he had in some time.

Eager to get rolling, he followed Josh from the room and they both quickly checked their weapons, ammo and supplies, grabbed their go bags and were out the door in short order.

Josh pulled up the directions on the GPS and Axel had the rental in gear before he was finished. As they exited Mile Road, Josh received a text.

"Holy shit. Jax and Dodge are on their way to the hospital. I'm going to be an uncle soon."

"Congratulations. Let's go find Bridget and the others so you can go home and meet your nieces or nephews or niece and nephew. Whatever."

Josh laughed. "Damn, I never dreamed I'd be this excited."

Axel smiled. He didn't have siblings, so he didn't know this feeling. But he now understood being part of something bigger than himself and being responsible for a human he was part of making. He relished the opportunity to be part of Aidyn's life. To help mold a human life.

The GPS sent updates and they both settled into their own thoughts while they drove. Within thirty-five minutes they were turning onto a country road. They drove past the driveway to the cabin to see if anything could be seen. The driveway was gravel, there were tall grasses on one side and woods on the other.

Stopping at the nearest driveway Axel turned the vehicle around and slowing inched down toward the driveway. Turning the headlights off on the vehicle, they both looked closely for any movement.

The sound of a smaller motor, racing toward them, could be heard and both men looked for any sign of the direction it was coming from. Axel put the vehicle in reverse and slowly backed up as they both scanned the trees. Finally, a headlight could be seen coming down the driveway around a bend.

They watched to see who would be on the four-wheeler. Both of them pulled their weapons and Josh got out of the vehicle and stood at the edge of the woods. Axel put the vehicle in drive and waited to see if he was going to have to chase the vehicle or if it would stop.

As it approached the end of the drive, Axel sat up straight and turned the headlights on the driver.

"Holy shit."

Slamming the vehicle in park, he jumped from the SUV only to have Bridget pull her weapon on him.

"Don't shoot. It's me, Axel."

"That will not prevent me from shooting you."

Josh stepped from the edge of the trees, hands up. "Bridget, it's Josh. We're here to bring you back."

Bridget seemed uncertain for a moment, then she lowered her weapon.

"There's more. About seven more as far as I can tell."

Axel stepped toward her, "Get in the car and we'll drive down and get them. Where are your captors?"

"One's dead, one unconscious."

"Is that all?"

"Yes. But there was at least a third man so there may be more coming in a van soon."

"Okay. Get in. We can't waste time."

She seemed hesitant. Josh then urged her along.

"Bridget. Leave the four-wheeler there. It may buy us some time if it's blocking the drive should someone come. Get in. Now."

She hopped off the four-wheeler and walked toward the rental. Axel stood still watching her. Bridget's eyes locked on his and held as she moved forward, and his heart hammered in his chest so hard it hurt.

Reaching the vehicle, she walked past him. Josh got into the SUV as Bridget said, "Thank you." Then opened the back driver's side door and climbed in.

Axel drove around the four-wheeler as best he could then

sped down the drive as Bridget instructed him on the curves.

"Are there more armed women?"

"Just one as far as I know. She's a student of mine."

Halfway up the drive Bridget said, "Stop here."

Axel stopped and Bridget got out of the truck and yelled.

"Come out. I've got a ride to get us out of here."

Women began coming out of the woods, crying, some hung back more fearful. As they neared the vehicle, Bridget opened the door and ushered them in. Some of them climbing into the back area. What he noticed about them all is they had blood and abrasions around their wrists. Some had bruises on their faces. They all looked scared and relieved at the same time.

The vehicle was crowded as they all piled in. None of them complained. Axel turned the vehicle around in the driveway and they headed out toward the road. The only sounds from the back were women crying and others consoling. Unfuckingbelievable.

Bridget sat directly behind him in the vehicle. When he looked into the rearview mirror he could see her face clearly. She sat next to the other woman with a gun and he wondered if she wanted to shoot him right now. Doubtful since she wanted him to get them all out of here.

As they weaved around the four-wheeler still parked at the end of the driveway and turned out onto the road, a white van met them. Bridget hissed from the backseat.

"That's them."

He looked back at them as they saw the four-wheeler in the driveway. Josh turned to watch them and said, "They're coming after us."

Some of the women cried louder, others screamed for them to go faster. Their terror was clear from their voices.

His eyes met Bridget's and he swallowed.

"We can't let them get away." He said it loud enough to be heard over the crying.

Josh pulled his phone out and called in to 911. Quickly relaying their location and the van he said, "Let them get closer so I can see the plates on the van."

Some of the women started screaming and Josh looked back at Bridget for help. He said, "We can't let them get away."

Bridget whistled loudly, which quieted everyone down. "Keep your heads down and shut up. They're right. If we let them get away, we'll always wonder if they're coming back." She turned to look to the back. "Sydney, you need to look at the license plates on the van and get what you can from them. Riah, you, too. Be your own saviors, ladies. We can do this."

She turned back to the front and her eyes caught his in the mirror. Josh continued talking on the phone and Axel slowed down while also grabbing his phone. One tap on the front of it and he was calling in to GHOST.

Ford answered. "What do you have, Axel?"

"A rental vehicle full of women who have been freed from a cabin in the woods and a van full of assholes..."

"Ukrainian assholes." Bridget interrupted.

"Ukrainian assholes on the chase. We're trying to get a tag on the plates and Josh is calling into local PD. We may need more assistance though."

He could hear keys tapping then Ford came back. "Let me see what I can do to get local PD to hurry. Where are you?"

He looked to Josh who quickly said, "West side of LaGrange County."

"You hear that Ford?"

"Roger. Hang tight."

The women started screaming and he could see the van speeding up. They meant to try and run them off the road. Josh yelled, "Brace, brace, brace."

Axel hit the gas and sped up before they were hit. Their best course of action now would be to get to the local police department.

25

Her heart raced for more reasons than one. He didn't look like a white knight, but at this moment he was her white knight. All of their white knights, he and Josh. She had a hard time not looking into the mirror at his eyes. They held so much in them. The hazel eyes that she was first so enamored with when she'd met him, but those same eyes stared at her every day. Those same eyes told her he loved her. The laughter in those hazel eyes when she tickled him. She'd thought of Axel almost every damned day since she found out she was pregnant. Even before that, after she'd left him at the hotel because she was scared. The time they spent was imprinted on her brain and now on her body. The few stretch marks and loosened skin on her belly reminded her every day of their night together.

Axel stepped on the gas and she was thrown back in the seat. They continued to speed down the road and soon the headlights behind them dimmed as the van seemed to lose speed or something happened to it.

"932CDT." One of the women yelled from the back.

Bridget was unsure if she wanted Axel to keep going or if she wanted him to slow down. What she did know, the last thing she wanted was to be captured again, because it would be worse this time. Her chances of escape would be out of the question.

Josh yelled, "Got it. Did you hear that, Ford?"

"Repeat."

"932CDT."

"Roger."

"I'll run them. Get the women to the police department to be interviewed. After that, they'll provide them with protection and counseling until these fuckers can be stopped."

"Roger. We have at least one down and one unconscious at the cabin. Can you alert local PD?"

"Roger."

Josh pressed the button on his phone and looked back to her.

"Did you hear that?"

"Yes."

She turned to the other women. "Who didn't hear that?"

No one spoke up. They were huddled together, four in the back and three plus herself scrunched together on the backseat.

She faced forward and saw Axel's eyes in the mirror. He

quickly looked back to the road and she turned her head to look out the side window. They had a long night ahead of them but the first thing she wanted to do was call her mom and find out how she and Aidyn were doing. Then she remembered that Sophie was sending a plane. Looking at Axel in the mirror she asked, "Did my mom and Aidyn get on a plane to Lynyrd Station?"

His eyes blazed into hers. They were harder now. Different. Almost scary.

"Yes."

She inhaled and looked out the window again. She wanted to ask to borrow his phone, but if they needed it for communication in case someone else accosted them or new information came in, she didn't want to tie it up. Plus, everyone else in the vehicle with her probably wanted to call home, too. She'd wait till they got to the police department.

Axel slowed down since it seemed they weren't being followed any longer. He turned onto the onramp to the highway smoothly and she allowed herself to relax for the first time in several hours. She still had a fair amount of adrenaline pumping through her veins, so she wasn't able to fully relax, but just giving her back a slight rest relieved some tension.

Jennie Lee sat stoically next to her saying nothing but slid her hand over to Bridget's and squeezed. Turning her hand so their fingers locked, Bridget squeezed hers back.

"Great work back there." Bridget whispered.

Jennie Lee said nothing, but soft sniffles reached her ears and rather than asking anything else Bridget simply leaned her head against Jennie Lee's. Solidarity. Support.

The slowing of the vehicle to exit the highway had her raising her head. Glancing out the window she saw they were almost to the police station and her heartbeat sped up once again. She tried running all the information through her mind so she wouldn't forget anything. She wanted...no she needed these men caught so she could sleep at night. They all needed that. None of them would ever feel safe again if they didn't stop these men and their sex trafficking ring. Being taken against your will is one of the most horrifying experiences a person can endure. The fact that they'd all gotten away was a miracle.

Two more turns and they were in the police parking lot. Axel parked the vehicle and the woman on the other side of the backseat opened the door immediately. Some of them smelled kind of bad, too. She'd just noticed that when the fresh air rushed in.

Opening her door and stepping out, she ran right into Axel who stood so close it was unnerving.

"Do you want to call them?"

His voice was tight, his posture was as well, but he held his phone out to her and she was anxious to call so she softly responded.

"Yes. Thanks."

Dialing her mom's number with shaking fingers she put Axel's phone to her ear and took two steps away so Jennie Lee could exit the vehicle.

Axel closed the driver's door and leaned back against it with his arms crossed over his chest. Sophie must have told him that Aidyn was his. He was clearly one pissed off man. Why that unnerved her she didn't know. She tried looking for Robert Beckman. He had no one to blame but himself.

"Hello?"

"Hi, Mom, I'm okay."

Tears rolled down her cheeks as her mom's sobs on the other end of the phone reached her ears.

"I'm so relieved. Oh my God, Bridget, I was so scared for you."

"I'm okay. They saved us. Axel and Josh did. How are you and Aidyn?"

She started shaking and her legs grew weak. She was afraid she'd fall over so she leaned against the squad car next to them. Her eyes watched as the other women were escorted into the police station, then she glanced at Axel who stood as he was before arms crossed watching her.

"We're fine. We're here right now with Roxanne and Yvette. They are playing hide and seek with Aidyn."

His little giggles could be heard over the phone and more tears streamed down her cheeks.

"Does he want to talk to me?"

"Aidyn, Momma's on the phone." her mom called.

So quickly his angelic little voice came on the phone.

"Hi, Momma. We're playing hide 'n seek. I'm winning. I'm a good finder Roxanne said."

"You are a good finder. I'm glad you're having fun."

"Are you coming to see us here. It's cool. They have a vator."

Her mom giggled. "An elevator."

"That's so cool. Soon honey, okay?"

"Okay."

"Let me talk to Momma, Aid."

Her mom got the phone and asked, "When will you be coming here? Did they catch the men that took you and the others? Are you safe?"

Bridget inhaled a deep breath to gather her composure.

"No, they haven't captured them. We just arrived at the police department and it'll likely be a while as we wait to be interviewed. I'll get back to you when I know what's going on."

"Oh, honey, I'm so relieved. Thank you for calling and hurry home."

"I will, Mom. I love you. Tell Aidyn."

"I will, sweetheart."

The line went dead, and she let out a long breath to calm herself. She handed the phone to Axel and pushed herself away from the squad car she leaned against to walk into the police station.

"I have a son?"

She froze. So, they were going to have this conversation now.

"Yes."

"You didn't tell me, and I'll assume that's because I told you my name was Robert Beckman."

"Yes." She ran her hands up and down her arms even though it was rather warm outside. "I looked for a Robert Beckman. I found you. You had a prison record and I figured we were better off without someone like you."

"I was undercover. The prison record was made up for that purpose."

"How do I know that to be true?"

"You can ask Gaige to pull up my records once we get to the compound."

"Won't he lie for you?"

He huffed out an irritated breath. "We don't lie about shit like that. What we do is dangerous. It's complicated sometimes. It's detailed all the time."

"You lied to me."

"Right. I'd just met you. What should I have said, 'Oh, by the way, I'm undercover this isn't my real name.' Then, if you were an operative working for the other side, you could have shot me dead."

"I wouldn't have...I wasn't..."

His voice raised. "How would I know?"

She raised her voice in response. "Do you always sleep with secret agents?"

He boomed. "No."

Realizing how loud he was, he scraped his hand through his long hair, and she was immediately sorry it had gotten this far.

His voice softened. "I was mesmerized by you. Captivated. Enthralled. You bewitched me. Then you left me. I came back at 8:00 as I said, and you'd disappeared. No last name. No note. No way to find you."

26

H e watched her eyes as he spoke, The fear was slipping away the farther they were from the cabin. The anger was slipping away, too. It wasn't all gone, but her eyes were softening to the eyes he remembered.

"I didn't..." She gently cleared her throat. "I didn't think you meant it. I didn't want to feel the fool and sit there and wait for you to come back. I thought you used that as an excuse to leave. I felt stupid for having slept with you."

"As I recall, we didn't sleep much."

She cocked her head, the overhead lights on the nearby lamppost shone on her reddish hair and created a halo around her head. The darkened area they stood in added shadowed effects to her face and her body, but still she was beautiful. Dirty but beautiful.

"Right. We didn't."

She ran her hands over her arms again and he decided this conversation could be finished later.

"Let's go inside. You'll need to be interviewed."

He stepped closer to her and she tilted her head up to look into his eyes briefly before turning and walking toward the entrance to the police department.

"Bridget, did you kill the dead captor at the cabin?"

"Yes."

Wow, that was impressive. She wasn't more than five feet tall, slender of build but capable as hell. As she turned he noticed the gun tucked in the waistband of her pants.

"You'll need to remove the magazine and bullet in the chamber from the weapon before you go in."

She stopped and pulled the gun from her back waistband with ease. Her nimble fingers easily removed the magazine, slid the rack back, as she tilted the weapon to the side and let the live round fall out. She absolutely was an expert with firearms, that much was apparent. She then held the pistol out for him to look down the slide and check for himself that it was unloaded. He looked down the barrel, slid his pinky in as far as he could and nodded. She then lay the pistol in her hand and held it out to him. He picked it up and carried it in with him, pointing it down to the ground as he entered.

Once inside, he lay it and the magazine on the counter of the desk, muzzle toward the wall, empty chamber up and nodded at the clerk.

"It's one of the Ukrainian kidnappers from the cabin these women were found at."

The clerk put on a rubber glove and catalogued the weapon, then lay it in an evidence box for the investigating officer to examine. Taking their names, he asked them to wait in the chairs against the wall.

They sat in silence for a long while, the other women had been escorted to individual rooms. It was procedure to interview each of them separately, so they didn't compare stories with each other.

"Is he a good boy?"

She smiled so sweetly before she answered. "He's so good. Smart. Happy. Amazing every day."

"From this point forward, I intend to be in his life. I'm so mad that I've missed this much of his life, I'll not miss anymore."

She inhaled deeply and stretched her shoulders back. "How do you intend to do that?"

"I don't have it all figured out yet. But I will. We will."

She nodded but said nothing else. He was mad. He was furious that he'd had a son for four and a half years or more and didn't know about him. All the times he'd dreamed of being a father. The betrayal of his former girlfriend and now this felt like a gut punch of the worst kind. The only saving grace is that he'd be able to make up for lost time hopefully. He'd be able to be there now if he could figure all of this out. He'd absolutely leave GHOST if he had to. Aidyn was so much more important to him than his job. He loved what he did, but not more than being a dad.

An officer walked around the counter, "Ms. Barnes, can you please follow me?"

She stood stiffly and he rose at the same time. She looked up at him and swallowed.

"Will you be here when I'm finished?"

"Yes."

She nodded and turned to follow the officer, but he reached out and grabbed her hand and squeezed it. Her beautiful green eyes looked deeply into his and a single tear slid down her right cheek before she squeezed his hand and let go. He stood watching her walk away until she disappeared behind a gray metal door.

He plopped down into the chair with a thud and Josh stepped in from outside with some packages in his hand. Sitting alongside him he held out two meal bars and a water.

"While you were checking Bridget in, I went out and raided my go bag."

Axel grinned at him and took one of the bars. "Thanks."

The foil wrapping seemed so loud in the quiet of the waiting area as he rotated his neck on his shoulders.

"So, you're a dad."

"Yeah."

"Unfuckingbelievable."

"Yeah."

Taking a bite from his bar, Josh's phone broke the silence.

"Masters."

Axel finished his meal bar and crumpled the package in his hand.

"No shit? That's fantastic. Is Jax okay?"

Josh's grin was huge. The joy on his face couldn't be denied. He'd have looked like that when Aidyn was born had he known. Things were different now and exactly how to tell Aidyn that he was his father started running through his mind. He'd follow Bridget's lead on that, but he wanted Aidyn to know as soon as possible. As soon as they got to GHOST.

"Hopefully we'll be back soon. We're at LeGrange PD now. Tell Jax I love her and congratulations."

Josh tapped his phone to end the call and then nudged him. "Bro, I now have a niece and nephew. Maya and Myles."

Axel held out his hand and shook his brother's hand. They were family, all of them, and their family had just grown by two more. Life would be very different from now on. The GHOST members were becoming parents, including him.

They sat quietly as Josh texted. Likely chatting with Jax or his mom or any number of family members they had around the country, the smile on his face immeasurable. After a few moments, Josh held out his hand to shake and

Axel's brows bunched together but he took Josh's hand and shook it.

"Congratulations, man, you became a father today."

Axel's stomach flipped and his heart raced and for the first time in a long time he felt elated to be called a father and not the heavy burden and anger of not knowing that all this time. From this point forward, he'd try to remember to look forward, not back.

A uniformed officer stepped out of the gray door Bridget had disappeared through, "Mr. Dunbar, can you follow me please?"

27

She answered question after question. She relayed information. Her story was told about five times over and over and her impatience grew with each time. It was procedure though, she did know that, but still it got on her nerves. She was tired and hungry, and she wanted to see her son. That didn't help her irritation one bit.

Finally, hours later, she was allowed to leave the station. Exhausted wasn't even close to a valid word for her present state. Her feet felt as if they had weights hanging on them and her vision was almost blurry.

An officer escorted her out of the hallway where the interrogation rooms were, and she was relieved to step into the hallway and see Axel still sitting there waiting for her.

Axel stood to his full height and his eyes watched her as she walked toward him. There was something about the way he looked at her now though that set her body tingling. When she neared him he stepped forward, the officer handed her a bag with her possessions in them, her cell phone and things that had been left in her vehicle and her range bag with her laptop in it.

Her arm dropped when taking her range bag, she'd not been prepared for the weight of it. Plus, her fatigue didn't help. She hated feeling helpless but was so grateful when Axel reached forward and took the heavy burden from her. He slung it over his shoulder and waited for her to say something.

First she addressed the officer. "Thank you."

The she turned to Axel. "Are you able to take me home?"

"Yes, that's why I waited." There was a bit of humor in his voice.

Two steps toward the door she stopped. "Hey, where's Josh?"

"I sent him to your place a few hours ago so he could sleep. Your mom gave us the keys and told us to feel free to stay while we were here looking for you. I figured if he slept now, when we get back, we can sleep, and he'll be rested enough to be on pseudo-guard duty. I wasn't sure how you would feel after what you've been through and felt the added security would help you rest. We have a plane coming for us all in the morning at 0800."

"Why? Won't Aidyn and my mom be coming back here?"

He stepped in front of her close enough that she had to tilt her head up to look into his eyes. "Bridget, we didn't get them. Not yet. They're still out there."

Her shoulders slumped forward and defeat consumed her, further weighing her down. "I thought police were on their way to the cabin to get them."

"All they found was a dead man."

Before she could gather her wits, tears streamed from her eyes. Angrily swiping at them she sniffed. "I'm tired."

He stepped aside, wrapped his right arm around her shoulders, which she allowed and enjoyed, and escorted her from the police department.

Stepping outside in the cool fresh air, she inhaled and enjoyed freedom. After all, she'd been captive for many hours, which by many standards was not long at all, and the enormity of how fortunate she was rained down on her. Tears flowed again but Axel said nothing at all. They walked across the parking lot to a vehicle that looked like hers. Wait, it was hers. Then she realized Josh had taken their vehicle and the police had hers here for forensic examination.

"They released it?"

"Yeah."

"What happened to the others?"

He chuckled lightly. "They've all been released and either had someone come and get them or hitched a ride to a hotel where the ladies from out of state have taken a couple of rooms together until they can get flights home."

"Will they be alright? Get counseling and such?"

"I don't know, honey. I did manage to find out that Skye's friend Riah has a husband who is anxious to have her back. Megan's friend, Carrie is going home to a husband who has been frantic and will see to her care and Yvette's friend, Bethany has parents to go home to. Jennie Lee and Sydney said they were bunking together for a while until they felt comfortable."

He opened the passenger door for her and waited for her to get in and buckle up. Closing the door once she was situated, she watched him walk around the front of her SUV to the driver's side. He was still handsome, even with that long hair, which she usually would balk at, but on him, it worked. She'd seen the hint of a long scar on his right cheek and remembered that he didn't have that when they were together.

He climbed in and his scent filled the SUV. It was calming and still sexy after a rather long day. He started the vehicle and began to drive her home and her mind frantically calculated where they'd all sleep. If Josh was there already, he was either sleeping in her mom's room or Aidyn's, which was kind of funny to think of because Aidyn's bed was far too small for him. So, likely he was in her mom's room, which left her, and Axel and Axel wouldn't fit in Aidyn's bed either. She could though. She'd do that, plus his pillow still smelled like him and she missed him terribly.

As Axel turned to merge onto the highway, she looked over at him. The scar ran along his cheek, just the tip of it showed, but she could see the end of it where his hair split further down his cheek.

"You didn't have that when we were together. What happened?"

"Knife fight."

She gasped. "My God."

"Five years ago, Wyatt and I got into a fight with a high knife-wielding guy. He was deranged and lashing at us. He was using his knife on Wyatt and I tried bringing him down. I got him off Wyatt. It ended up that he got both of us. Wyatt's scar is on the other cheek and goes down his neck. I guess I was lucky."

She watched him swallow, then unconsciously move his hair so it covered it.

"Does it make you uncomfortable?"

His eyes left the road to lock on hers a moment, then back to the road. His Adam's apple bobbed as he swallowed, and she already knew the answer and her heart hurt for him.

"Yes."

It was barely audible, but she heard it.

"Were you on duty?"

"Yes."

His jaw clenched and his teeth ground slightly, that soft little sound you can hear when someone grinds their teeth. Aidyn did it in his sleep sometimes. Like his father.

Axel turned into her driveway and relief flooded her body at the thought of a shower and sleep.

28

They walked up to the front door, but Axel touched her shoulder.

"Hang on. We don't want to get shot. Let me text Josh."

His fingers typed as fast as he could. He struggled sometimes with his fingers hitting the wrong keys, but he typed carefully and was rather proud about how he managed his message.

"We're here now and entering the house."

"I heard you and looked out the window."

Turning his phone, he showed Bridget that they were safe to go in and she smiled and opened the front door. She sighed when they entered the living room and he almost did, too. It was nearing 4:00 a.m. and he'd had little sleep last night.

"I'm going to take a shower then I'll sleep in Aidyn's room, I don't think you'll fit. If you need to use the bathroom first go ahead."

"Thanks, I can wait till you're finished."

"Okay. Make yourself at home. I won't be long."

He watched her disappear down the hall and wanted to see if there was a beer in the fridge and relax, but it was likely not safe until they got out of here so that would wait until tomorrow. Flopping down on the sofa instead, he glanced over and saw his go bag laying on the floor next to it.

"I brought it in for you." Josh stood against the wall, arms crossed, his dark hair messed from sleep. He wore jeans and a t-shirt, just in case.

Axel smiled at him. "Thanks. All quiet here?"

"Yeah."

"Any word on the Ukrainians?"

"Nothing yet. The dead one is being identified. He has a strange tattoo on his back right shoulder of a sickle, hammer and a fist twisted together. Ford is running it through the database looking for affiliation logos. Gaige and Sophie had a baby boy."

Axel chuckled. "I wondered where Gaige had gone off to. Everyone doing okay?"

"Yeah. I guess they named him Tate."

Axel sat back into the sofa and scrubbed his hands through his hair. "That seems fitting and a great tribute to

Tate Turner." Tate Turner was Sophie's brother and Gaige's best friend for years. He'd died while on duty in the Army and both of them missed him terribly.

"Yeah. Place is filling up with kids, man. I'm going back to bed for a bit. Plane will be here at 8:00 a.m."

"Night." Axel looked at his phone and saw that it was ten minutes after 4 a.m. They weren't going to get a ton of sleep, but maybe he'd just set his alarm and take his shower before they left the house.

Pushing himself off the sofa with a slight groan, he made his way back to Bridget's bedroom. Kicking his boots off next to the bed, he took his side arm out from its holster and lay it on the table, stretched out on top of the covers, set his phone alarm, lay his phone next to his side arm and listened to the water running in the shower. It wasn't long before he was asleep.

The bed dipping woke him with a start, his immediate reaction was to reach for his gun, but Bridget's voice came to him immediately.

"I'm friendly. Can I lay here? I guess I feel insecure in the other room and as tired as I am, I'm hearing noises that aren't there and just want to be next to you."

His eyes slightly adjusted to the light in the room, the sun was not up yet, though it would be soon. Stretching out his right arm to the side, Bridget climbed up the foot of the bed and lay in the crook of his arm.

Instinctively, he wrapped his arm around her and pulled her tightly to his body. She was stiff as she lay against him.

"Look Bri, you need to relax. Plane will be here in about 3 hours. Josh and I are here. If someone tries anything, we'll be here to protect you."

He squeezed her to him and held tight until he felt her relax against him. What a feeling that was. Unbelievable. They fit together amazingly.

He relaxed his body and waited until he heard her deep even breathing. It didn't take long. Thank God because he was exhausted.

He'd be meeting his son in a few hours. Actually, meeting him and he was eager to spend time with him. That led him to thoughts of what a four-year-old did for fun. What was his favorite color? Did he watch cartoons? Which were his favorites? Did he play games? Which ones? What was his favorite food? What did he like to do first thing in the morning? Did he go to school yet? Some schools offered 4K school, and Aidyn would be old enough for that. The questions kept popping into his head and he couldn't wait to find out the answers to each of them.

Then, the biggest question of all popped into his head. What would they do now? The thought of him living in Lynyrd Station while Aidyn and Bridget were here made his stomach turn. He wanted to be with his son. He wasn't ready to leave GHOST. He could if he wanted to, he had more than enough money. But, what would he do? And, would he and Bridget live in the same house or would they live separately? They weren't a couple, but he wanted to be there every day when Aidyn woke up. He'd missed so much time already, he didn't want to miss another day.

Finally, the questions stopped barraging his brain and he felt his body relax fully and knew sleep would finally come soon. The last thought he had was that Bridget felt so good laying against him. Her head lay on his right shoulder, her right arm rested comfortably on his chest and her hair smelled amazing. Simply amazing.

29

A blaring sound pierced her deep sleep, and it wouldn't stop. Finally, movement next to her had her eyes flying open and she sat up abruptly and looked down at the man lying next to her.

Axel's eyes looked into hers and held for a long time. His full, sensual lips finally turned up into a slow sexy smile. "Morning."

"Morning." She lay back down on her back staring at the ceiling as the memories of yesterday flooded her brain.

"I'm going to take a shower if you don't mind. We have to get on the plane in 45 minutes. You'll need to pack some clothes to stay for a while."

"Why are we staying with you?"

"We don't have word yet that the Ukrainians have been found and we can't leave you here in case they come back. We're not sure why they're targeting women who are friends with our women whose husbands are in GHOST, but we've got some work to do and it's my job to keep you and Aidyn safe. Of course, your mom as well."

"How in the hell do you think it's your job to keep us safe?"

She bolted upright and looked over at him as he stood and grabbed his phone and gun off the nightstand. Was he for real? She never had anyone else 'keep' her safe. That was her job.

"You are the mother of my child. My son. I take that very seriously. I don't want anything to happen to any of you."

"I can take care of myself. And Aidyn. And, my mom."

He stopped what he was doing and stared at her and her heart beat increased. His brows furrowed then he shook his head slowly.

"Really? Was what happened yesterday you taking care of yourself?"

"How dare you."

She scooted off the end of the bed and stood to face him.

"If it weren't for your group, no one would be targeting people that know you all."

He took a step toward her and the hard edge his face formed was scary. That was probably what guys saw when he brought them down.

"You were followed to and through the airport. Two women you know were taken. You put yourself in a position to be taken despite all the warnings. I don't call that taking care of yourself. And, what about our son?"

Now she was mad. Her voice rose and her temper flared. "I'd never do anything to harm my son."

"I didn't say you would do anything to harm him. Intentionally. But you let your guard down, Bridget. You weren't aware of your surroundings. What do you teach your clients when they come to you for training?"

His voice boomed right back at her and that last shot, well that one hurt. 'Cause he was right. Dammit. She'd tell them no matter where they were to always be aware. She went to the range to pack up because they were going to a safer place than here and she let her guard down.

Angry, hurt tears blurred her vision. Her heart raced; her fists were tucked as tightly as they'd ever been. He took a step back and lowered his voice.

"I'm good at my job. I'm great at my job. As are all of my co-operatives. Protection is ingrained in each of us, 24-7 as are other skills you don't even want to know about. Protection is only one thing we do for total strangers. You are not a stranger to me. Aidyn is my blood as much as yours. While he is a stranger to me in some ways, he's as much my responsibility as yours. And, make no mistake, I will protect you two. I will ensure my family is safe."

He bent down and snagged a duffle bag off the floor and exited the room without another word. She watched the empty door frame for a few moments, then plopped down on the foot of the bed and let out a long sigh. She'd always had to rely on herself and after Aidyn came along, she was the sole parent and responsible party for him. Alone. It was clear now that Axel knew about Aidyn, he'd not be denied his parental responsibility. He was as fierce as she was right now and that was both disconcerting and comforting. To say there was an adjustment period coming was an understatement. Coming? Hell, the adjustment period was here, and her head spun with the magnitude of what that actually meant.

Closing her eyes and taking in a deep breath, counting to ten, then slowly releasing it, she opened her eyes and decided that little sleep and an argument first thing in the morning was not the way to start the day. So, for now, while she felt weakened and vulnerable, she'd go to Lynyrd Station with Axel and Josh and she'd spend some time with Sophie and Aidyn and her mom, and they'd hopefully figure things out between them as to how this would work moving forward.

Standing and walking to her closet, she grabbed some jeans, t-shirts, socks, undergarments and an extra pair of tennis shoes in case her boots weren't good enough to wear. She also grabbed a couple of dresses and heels just in case. Pulling her suitcase from the back of the closet she stood and looked at the picture of her and Axel, taken after they'd had sex so many years ago. Both of them smiling and looking quite satisfied. Her skin glowed and she looked happy.

Turning to lay the suitcase on the bed, she began packing her clothing and her purse; her hair products were in the bathroom, but she'd have to run in there to grab her toothbrush and other personal products anyway.

Looking over at her desk, she saw her laptop laying on top and wondered if her work laptop was in her range bag that Axel and carried for her yesterday. She'd have to ask because she'd need it to contact her clients about classes being cancelled.

Dropping her laptop into her suitcase, she grabbed a few hair ties and other items and dropped them in as well. The bathroom door opened, and she held her breath in case Axel came back into this room. Slight disappointment weighted on her chest when he didn't but instead went out to the living room where she heard him talking to Josh.

She went into the bathroom and brushed her teeth. Then she gathered the items she'd need, placed them into the suitcase, zipped it up and set it on the floor. Grabbing her boots from where she'd left them last night, she put them on and laced them up; she grabbed a cardigan from her closet and put it on. She was slightly cool this morning. Presumably because of the need to eat and sleep.

Feeling ready she wheeled her suitcase to the living room where Josh and Axel sat talking waiting for her. They both stopped and looked at her, Josh then broke the silence.

"Morning."

"Morning." She looked at Axel. "Do you know if my work computer is still in the back of my vehicle or if the police have it at the station? I need it to contact my clients."

"It's in your vehicle. They released it yesterday."

He seemed calmer now and he smelled amazing. His hair was still damp and combed in a way as to cover the scar on his cheek, and she felt sorry that he was so self-conscious about it. He was an incredibly handsome man, even with the scar.

He stood then. "Ready? We've got to meet the plane."

30

They'd all been quiet on the ride to the airport. Sleep deprivation did that at times, so did awkward situations. He parked the SUV alongside the hangar where the rental car company would come and pick it up. Climbing out of the vehicle, they extracted their bags from the back and he and Bridget followed Josh into the hangar and onto the GHOST plane.

He watched Bridget's reaction to each new location and once they'd reached the inside of the plane she turned to look at him.

"You really meant a private plane."

"Yes, it's Gaige's plane."

Josh flopped into a seat on the left side of the aisle where there wasn't a table between his seat and the seats ahead of him. His head immediately lay back on the headrest, but Axel knew as soon as the plane took off, he'd recline his seat and get a few winks, though it would be a short doze since it was only about an hour flight.

Axel motioned with his right hand for Bridget to sit next to the window, facing toward the front of the plane and he stowed her luggage and his go bag in the luggage area near their seats securing the bags from bouncing around.

He then sat in the seat next to Bridget and buckled his seatbelt. She watched him and quickly did the same.

The door closed and Gavin appeared at the front. "All ready to take off?"

"Yes, we're all set." Axel responded. He turned to look at Josh who didn't even open his eyes. Looking back at Gavin, he shrugged, and Gavin nodded once and turned to the cockpit disappearing inside.

"Private pilot, too?" Bridget said aloud but not necessarily to him or anyone.

"Yep."

The engines started and the plane exited from the back of the hangar, taxiing toward a runway. They never concerned themselves with the details since Gavin was highly capable. They stopped at the opening of a runway, for only a few moments.

"We've been cleared for takeoff." Sounded over an intercom and Axel rested his head against the backrest much like Josh.

The plane soon moved again, and they entered the runway, then accelerated for lift off. He closed his eyes as they lifted off the ground.

Once they'd leveled off, Gavin's voice came throughout the plane trip. "Weather is great, no issues ahead, we should have a smooth flight and land in 47 minutes."

He glanced over at Bridget who stared out the window, the sun shining through lit her hair and made it look like molten copper. Shiny and fiery. It was longer than it had been when they'd been together and the length suited her. It waved here and there and softly fell over her slender shoulder.

She turned her head to see him staring at her and his cheeks heated.

She smiled slightly. "I'm sorry for my temper flare this morning. I'm tired, edgy and I feel out of control of my life. Also, I'm nervous about introducing you to Aidyn as his father."

He nodded. "I'm sorry, too. Same. I'm trying so hard not to be angry about not knowing Aidyn was born. I've been fighting the feeling of all that I missed and being pissed at you and myself. We both screwed up, Bridget."

"I know. I should have given you my name and I shouldn't have been afraid of being played. But I did look for you under the name you'd given me." He didn't say anything understanding her thinking. She picked at a piece of invisible lint on her thigh then turned to face him. "What do you do exactly?" Her hand waved around as if taking in the entire plane. "As in a job. Clearly nasty men are after you by proxy. You have a private plane. A compound and money. Sophie only told me security. This is far from security."

Her voice shook a bit and he felt sorry for her. It was a lot to take in. "We are security but on a different level than bodyguards or building security. GHOST is an elite civilian special forces team. We're hired by the government for tasks they can't do. Not everything we do is completely legal. But we get our assignments through our contact in the State Department and often work with a military contact who reports to the State contact. Sometimes because of them and sometimes not, we usually have good luck getting local law enforcement to work with us when they realize we're there to help them. We sometimes have civilian clients, too. Our clients pay top dollar because what we do is dangerous and off the books, if you will."

He watched her closely and she swallowed a lump in her throat as she nodded slowly and looked at that stubborn piece of lint on her thigh.

"Look, we live in the compound because it's safe there. Some of my team members live in their own houses not far away and have security in place. It's even more so now that children are involved. We have resources, money and connections. That doesn't mean we aren't put in positions, such as this, where someone wants to make us pay. We'll get to the bottom of this though so we can all feel safe again. But I can tell you this. There is not one of my teammates that wouldn't drop whatever they are doing to help another out. That includes Sophie and Jax. Dedication is key and we are all dedicated."

His phone pinged a text around the same time as Bridget's. They both reached for their phones and he saw a text from Gaige. A picture of Gaige, Sophie and baby Tate filled his screen. They looked blissfully happy.

He chuckled as he looked at this picture and swallowed the anger that tried to rise again that he would never have a picture like this of him, Bridget and Aidyn.

"Tate is fitting for his name. Sophie told me if it had been a girl they'd have named her Kate."

"Yeah. The best way to remember someone you love that is gone is to name the person you love more than life after them. They continue to live on that way."

"Yeah. Aidyn is named after my grandfather."

He turned to stare into her gorgeous green eyes. In this light they looked like the new grass in the summer. So pure and bright and absolutely stunning with the backdrop of her fiery red hair.

"That's nice." He inhaled deeply and let it out slowly.

Bridget reached over and took his hand in hers. "Aidyn's middle name is Robert." She swallowed. "I thought that was your name."

His eyes watered and he closed them and lay his head against the headrest. A tear slowly slid down his left cheek and he angrily swiped at it, then he told himself to get some rest, he was as emotional as a teenage girl.

31

Pulling into the driveway of the compound was a huge surprise. First of all, the word compound sounded like an Army barracks with bland gray walls. This was a gorgeous southern mansion with all its opulence and charm.

Axel turned right at the top of the driveway and hit a garage door button which opened a door which wasn't a garage at all. He entered, closed the door with the same button on his visor, and they descended to a lower level, the drive circling around down not one but two levels below ground.

At the bottom they drove into a well-lit white garage filled with vehicles. Some spaces were left open, but many were filled, and she marveled at all the vehicles. Each one neat and clean, the garage itself kept tidy and not like a garage at all.

Axel parked his truck and jumped out, first opening the backdoor for her, then walking back to grab their bags.

Josh hopped out and took his bag and headed toward an elevator door to their left.

"This must be the elevator that Aidyn was so excited about."

Axel chuckled. "Yeah. It's rather impressive here."

The elevator doors opened and they each stepped in. Josh asked, "Which floor?"

"Second floor. I'll show Bridget where Jax's old room is and we'll figure out where everyone is going to sleep."

Josh reached forward and tapped the number 2 and the elevator doors slowly closed and began to rise out of the ground level.

She looked at the number panel and saw, "Garage", "Conf.", "1" and "2". Four levels of space here in this house. You'd never know from the outside.

Axel must have been watching her face. "We purposely didn't want to draw a lot of attention to this house so the outside looks like it may have looked when built. Beautifully restored. But, we had these underground levels dug and built to hold operations which can also be locked down should we ever come under attack. We have a medical clinic, gun range, workout facility and our operations room on the Conference level. On the first floor is the main level from outside. The kitchen, dining room, Gaige's office, formal living room and large foyer area are located there. The second floor is where all of our personal rooms are. Though with Gaige and Sophie now having Tate, and no doubt more to come, I assume some remodeling will take place. Wyatt and Yvette have purchased the old house next door to the south and are remodeling it for themselves and for Wyatt to perhaps take on more of the office type work and less of the field work. They're building an underground garage and a tunnel leading to this house. I imagine, Gaige and Sophie will commandeer Wyatt's rooms here for babies. As we bring on new members, another property will have to be purchased."

"Wow. That's amazing." She was trying to not be impressed but it was difficult not to be.

The elevator stopped at the second floor and they all stepped off and turned to the right. Josh walked ahead and unlocked the second door on the left. "I'm getting some shut-eye. I'll see you at supper."

Axel stopped at the first door and nodded as Josh disappeared. Then he knocked on the door they stood in front of. "These are Jax's former rooms. Your mom and Aidyn are staying in here."

The door opened and her mom gasped. "Oh, Bridget."

She was quickly wrapped in her mother's arms and she immediately felt a bit better. Then Aidyn came running across the room and jumped into her mom and her. She giggled and bent down to lift Aidyn and to wrap her little boy in her arms. His arms wrapped tightly around her neck and he nuzzled his face there. This made her feel a hundred times better. Absolutely.

After she'd hugged him as long as he'd allow, she bent down and set his feet on the floor, then turned to Axel and took in a deep breath.

"Aidyn, I'd like you to meet Axel. Axel is your father."

"You said I didn't have a daddy."

"I never said that. I said your daddy wasn't around. But, I was wrong. He is. He's right here."

Axel knelt and looked at Aidyn's precious little face as he processed this new information.

"You're my daddy?"

"I am."

"Why didn't you come to my birthday party?"

"I surely would have had I known about it. I will absolutely be there for every single birthday from this point forward though."

Aidyn stared at Axel for a while, then he looked up at her. "You didn't vite him to my party?"

"I didn't know where he was, Aid. It's a hard story to tell you, but I didn't know how to find him to tell him about you. He didn't know you were born until this week and I'm so very sorry I didn't know how to contact him. But, from now on we know where he is, and he knows where we are, and we'll all be together at all your birthdays and Christmas and all the holidays."

"Because you married?"

Oh my God. "Oh, honey, no, we're not married. But we know how to find each other now."

Aidyn's little brows furrowed a bit, then he turned and looked at Axel. And the similarities between them were striking and numerous.

"Do you know how to play Mario?"

"No, but I'd love it if you taught me how to play."

"'K. You have to sit over here, and we have to keep the sound low, Gramma wants to hear things."

Axel laughed and looked up at her, a softness in his face she hadn't seen since that picture of them in her closet. Wow.

32

He still didn't know how to play Mario. He'd never been a gamer, but he did have fun and so did Aidyn. He laughed at Axel's inability to touch the correct buttons at the right time. In his defense, Axel's fingers were much bigger than Aidyn's and more suited for pulling a weapon than playing a video game. But, he still made the effort. If for no other reason than to just enjoy time with his son. His son. His son. He'd never get tired of saying that. Bridget had lay on the bed in the room and fell fast asleep. Vivian had gone down and gotten them a snack when she'd asked Axel the last time he had a meal and he told her a meal bar at the police station. She'd tsked, then went downstairs and brought him scrambled eggs, a freshly baked muffin, coffee and juice. She'd brought Aidyn the same only in a smaller portion and for Bridget, just the muffin, cream cheese and fruit since she was sleeping. Eggs wouldn't taste very good cold and she wanted to allow Bridget time to sleep. As for Axel after they'd finished eating, he knew he should sleep, but he didn't want to. Not until Vivian told him it was nap time.

Aidyn balked a little, but Axel tried soothing his mood.

"My room is just across the hall." He opened the door and pointed to his room. "I'll leave the door unlocked so you can come in when you wake up. Deal?"

Aidyn looked across the hall and thought about it for a moment. Vivian then added, "Aidyn, Momma missed you. Why don't you snuggle up next to her for your nap and you'll both help the other sleep?"

"Okay." His innocent little face, so familiar to his own turned up to his. "I have to help Momma sleep. See you when I get up."

"Sounds good little man."

He watched as Aidyn climbed up on the bed and snuggled against Bridget, whose arms instantly opened to fold him into her body. A soft smile played on Bridget's face, but her eyes never opened. He couldn't wait until he'd be able to cradle Aidyn in his arms like that.

He stepped out of the room, gently closing the door with a final glance at his son, took a deep breath and walked across the hall. His go bag lay next to his door. He scooped it up and dropped it inside the door to deal with later. Now that the nap had been arranged, it called its siren song to him and he only wanted to sleep.

Kicking his boots off and flopping on his bed his eyes barely closed before he was out.

***

Movement on the bed had his eyes flying open only to see a much younger version of his face right up to his.

Axel smiled. "Hey. Did you have a good nap?"

"Yeah. There's a baby here." The excitement in his voice was undeniable.

"There is? What's his name?"

"Tate."

"Wow. Where is Tate now?"

Aidyn scurried off the bed and grabbed Axel's hand. "Come on, I'll show you."

Axel laughed and followed Aidyn out into the hall and down the grand staircase. He could hear the women cooing and chatting and a very proud Gaige stood just outside the ring of women circling his wife and child. Gaige's eyes met his and the smile on his face was one of pure joy. Then Gaige's eyes landed on Aidyn and his smile grew a bit more.

At the bottom of the steps, Gaige walked over to meet them and shook Axel's hand. He softly said, "Congratulations."

"Congratulations to you as well." He looked down at Aidyn still holding his hand. "Have you met my son, Aidyn?"

"Not formally. I only saw him in passing." Gaige leaned down and held his hand out to shake Aidyn's.

Aidyn smiled broadly and shook Gaige's hand. "It's nice to meet you, Aidyn."

"Axel is my dad."

"I've heard that. You're lucky to have Axel as a dad. He's rock solid and genuinely a good person."

"He is?"

"Yep. He's lucky to have you, too."

Aidyn nodded. "Can I see the baby?"

Gaige chuckled. "Sure, come on over."

Gaige walked to Sophie and kissed her on the temple.

"We have a little man here to meet Tate."

Sophie started to bend down but Axel held his hand out to stop her. Leaning down he scooped Aidyn up in his arms so he could see Tate easier. Plus, bonus, he got to hold Aidyn in his arms. Bridget moved to stand alongside, and he looked down at her and smiled. When she smiled back it hit him right in the heart. Bam. Just like that.

"He's little. Not me, I'm big." Aidyn stated proudly.

The group gathered around, his friends and co-operatives laughed, and his heart was full.

Gaige received a text. Reading it, the look on his face went from proud papa to business mogul. His eyes first caught Wyatt's then his. He jerked his head toward the elevator and Axel knew it was time to work.

Glancing at his son, who was so enthralled with Tate made him fall in love a little more. Is that how it was? You loved them when you had them, but then each sweet, cute, adoring thing they did made you love them more and in a different way?

"Hey, Bud, I have to go downstairs to work for a little bit. I'll see you soon, okay?"

"But, you'll come back? Today. Not for a long time?"

Aidyn's brows bunched together, and he stepped away from the crowd to have a moment with him. It would be natural that Aidyn would wonder or worry since he hadn't been around him until now. Walking over to the staircase, he sat on the second from the bottom step and sat Aidyn on his lap. Bridget followed them and sat alongside him.

"Hey, I know I didn't know how to find you before, but I do now. And, we're all right here in this house. Sometimes I have to go to work for a day or two at a time, but when that happens, I'll call you every day. For right now though, this is just a meeting in the conference room downstairs to share information. I'll be back up in a little while, okay?"

Aidyn thought for a long time about his words. Axel didn't break eye contact with him though, he wanted him to know he was serious. Finally, Bridget soothed Aidyn's fears as only a mother can do.

"Hey, Aid. We have daddy in our lives now and nothing will change that. You can help me take care of Sophie and Tate because Tate's daddy has to go to work with your daddy. So, we'll help little Tate be happy and Tate will help us be happy. Okay?"

"Okay." Aidyn looked into Axel's eyes and said, "I'll see you later. I have to help Tate."

Then he scrambled off Axel's lap and ran into the back dining room where the ladies were still gathered together chatting.

Bridget stood and stepped off the steps turning to face him.

"Thank you for playing with him and letting me sleep earlier."

"You don't have to thank me. I had a great time being with him."

"Yeah. He's pretty great."

They stared into each other's eyes for a few moments and his emotions were all over the board. He still held some resentment that she'd left him so many years ago, that he'd not gotten her name and that she had his baby without him knowing about it. In fairness, she couldn't give him his real name. She'd also done a fantastic job raising him alone while building a business and all the other stressors that came along with parenthood.

And, she was still beautiful. Her clear green eyes looked into his and he swore he could see her soul in them.

"I better let you go." She turned and walked to the dining room behind the grand staircase, and he heaved out a deep breath and headed toward the elevator to see what information Gaige had received.

33

She still felt uneasy and, of course, creeped out when thoughts barraged Bridget of her recent ordeal. The women in the house were great about not saying anything, unless she wanted, but Skye, Megan, Roxanne and Yvette were texting friends as they chatted and from their expressions, she guessed who they were texting and what it was about.

Sitting at the dining room table with her mom, Sophie and Tate, Roxanne, Yvette, Megan and Shelby, who was sleeping peacefully in her mama's arms, and Skye, Bridget looked at the women gathered and was impressed and awed by them. Of course, Jax was missing, having just had twins, she was resting at home with her mother, Pilar, helping out. Aidyn was sitting between Bridget and Sophie, staring at Tate. He was mesmerized by Tate. Then he'd look over and stare at Shelby sleeping in Megan's arms and watch her for a while, then turn to look at Tate again. After a half hour he said he was bored so Vivian took him upstairs to play games for a little while.

A few minutes later, Axel appeared in the doorway and searched the room for Aidyn. His brows furrowed but before he could ask she said, "My mom took him upstairs. He was bored."

His shoulders visibly relaxed then his eyes bored into hers.

"I need you to come downstairs, Bridget."

"Is everything alright?"

"I'll explain everything downstairs."

The look of worry on his face scared the crap out of her and as she stood her knees threatened to shake uncontrollably.

Sophie looked at her. "We're all right here if you need anything."

The other women nodded, and she swallowed and mumbled, "Thank you."

Bridget tried practicing calming breathing as she walked beside Axel down the hallway and to the elevator. She knew there was a floor one, but she'd never have guessed this was it. The doors looked exactly like the rest of the doors in the home. Stepping inside she blew out a breath.

"You're scaring me."

"I'm not trying to, Bridget. I'm not at liberty to share this information with you until we are in the conference room."

"Okay."

He reached over and took her hand in his and squeezed and she almost cried. What she wouldn't give for an honest to goodness hug right now. It had been so long. Aidyn hugged her, of course, and so did her mom, but Axel's would be different, his smell, the feel of his body next to hers, the deep timber of his voice as he whispered in her ear, his strength. All of it. She wanted a hug.

It was as if he was thinking the same thing 'cause he half turned to face her and she did the same thing. He bent slightly and pulled her in his arms and wrapped them tightly around her and she came undone.

The tears came at blinding speed as she wrapped her arms as tightly as she could around his shoulders. His arms squeezed her tighter and it was as if a wound was being healed. Hundreds of thousands of times she'd thought of him over the years. Every time Aidyn laughed he looked like his father. Every time Aidyn said, "I'm hungry." she thought of Axel, actually, Robert, but him. Even after she found out he was in prison, she wondered why and if he'd get out and look her up. She'd forgotten she hadn't given him her name, her last name. All this time she'd hoped to see him again, not even remembering he wouldn't know how to find her.

Right now, with his arms wrapped around her, he stood and lifted her feet off the floor and the feeling was akin to what she though heaven would be like.

He whispered in her ear, "It's going to be alright. I'm here for you and Aidyn and we'll get through all of this. Then, we'll figure out what we do from here, okay?"

All she could do was nod against his head so he knew she heard, but she couldn't speak right now. Not without sounding like a blabbering fool. She sniffed as the elevator slowed its decent. Axel squeezed her one more time then let her slide down his body. She took a step back and looked into his eyes. He swiped under her eyes with his thumbs and smiled softly.

"I'm here, okay?"

"Yeah." She huffed out a breath and let it out slowly.

Inhaling she turned to the doors as they opened, and Axel waited for her to step out into the hallway before stepping out. He pointed down the hall and began walking toward the door with the frosted glass door, lit from the inside.

Reaching the door, he opened it and stood back, allowing her to enter first. There she saw the male members of GHOST, except for Dodge. Everyone else was present and nodded at her as she entered.

Gaige spoke first and he pointed to a chair to his left, "Take a seat, Bridget."

Axel pulled out her chair and she sat, her back stiff, her emotions teetering on the edge and her composure, barely existent.

Axel sat next to her and lay his forearms on the table, folding his hands together then tucking them under his chin. Gaige tapped some of the keys on his laptop and then turned to face her.

"I'm sorry to have to share this news with you, Bridget."

34

He watched her process her nervous energy while waiting to hear what Gaige had to say. She was impressive.

Gaige said, "We've received a call from Stueben PD. We got the call because I've been in contact with the Chief there and told him you were staying with us here. That said, I'm sorry to tell you that your house and range, Armed and Dangerous, were burned to the ground today. They are still working on the forensics in both locations, and they will let us know when there is more information. Between us, we believe the Ukrainians came back to find you and when you weren't around, they decided to teach you a lesson. No one was harmed. Property damage only. So, before you say anything, please know you, Aidyn and your mom are welcome to stay here as long as you need to, so as to where you'll live, you've got options."

Her lips quivered but she straightened her shoulders, sucked in a deep breath and let it out slowly.

"So, it's time to pull up my big girl pants and face this head on. I have insurance on both my house and my business. I can rebuild, change course or do nothing. Nothing isn't an option, so I'll figure the rest out. I have my business laptop, so I can contact my clients to keep them up to date and there is no doubt as soon as I'm open again, I'll have my business back."

Leaning forward she said, "Okay. Now that I've talked all that out, where do we begin to find these assholes?"

Gaige looked around the room at everyone and grinned. They were no doubt worried she'd burst out crying and there wasn't a man in the room, including himself, that could handle a woman crying. Even Josh, though he pretended he was immune to it.

"Well, Bridget, this is our problem. For some reason they are targeting women close to our group. We're working on it."

"Well, while they've done that, they've made it my business."

She turned her head toward Axel and locked eyes with him. "I'm not going to stop until I know my family is safe. I will not live in fear. I've done incredibly hard things in my life. I'm trained in weaponry, I'm capable and I'm smart. They've messed with the wrong person this time."

"Okay, but, Bridget, we can't go off half-cocked, we have to devise a plan. We're still gathering information on these guys and until we have that, we have to play with our brains not our brawn."

She nodded. "I get it. But, I plan to be in on this. I want my revenge."

He looked up at Gaige and waited for some signal that he'd allow her to do something in this mess to help her feel as though she got her revenge. It was hard living the rest of your life feeling like you were unable to get closure. He wanted that for her. For them, because like it or not, they had a common goal in life for the rest of their lives and that was to make sure Aidyn was safe, healthy and secure.

Gaige nodded slightly and he relaxed a bit. Gaige's phone rang and he answered promptly. He looked around the table and held up his hand silently asking them to hold tight, he was getting some intel.

Leaning close to Bridget he tried not smelling her perfume but couldn't. He whispered, "We're getting some intel now, but we can't do anything until we work it up through Gaige and we are all on the same page. That way, no one gets hurt."

"Okay."

Gaige's call ended. "Okay, here's what we have right now. The Ukrainian at the cabin was Fedir Bulikov. He's part of the resistance movement in the Ukraine called, VNSK which stands for control Vzyaty Na Sebe Kontrol or Assume Control. They are kidnapping and selling women on the black market to make enough money to fund their resistance operation. The other man in the cabin that was working with him is Victor Boyko. He's still in the wind though PD did find identifying information for him in the cabin. They had been using that as their home base here in Indiana. They haven't identified the third man yet. Both Victor and Fedir work for the mastermind of the operation, Mikheil Ustymovych."

Lincoln spoke next, "Do we know how big this selling operation is here in the US? And, do we know why they're targeting friends of our wives?"

"No, not yet." Gaige looked around the room. "Guesses?"

Wyatt sat forward, his jaw tight. "I have a theory if we can put the two together. John Caulfield was doing the same thing, kidnapping women and selling them. We thought when he was killed that operation was over. What if we were wrong?"

Axel said, "What if Caulfield was kidnapping for Ustymovych? We stopped that operation. It would make sense they would be pissed at us."

Ford leaned forward and put his arms on the table. "The only way they'd know about us is if Caulfield told them where we were when he was stalking us. Yvette had information from him that he knew was damming, we thought it was his own skin he was worried about. Maybe we stopped digging too soon. If we can find what Caulfield was really worried about Yvette having knowledge of, we just may find the links to Ustymovych."

Axel sat back in his chair contemplating all of this information. "The man we got when we found Caulfield may be able to give us some information. Is he still in prison?"

His wheels were turning. His heart raced; excitement coursed through him as he contemplated the hunt. This was the part of the job that excited him the most.

Pulling the information together and coming up with the plan.

Bridget turned to look at him, her face had confusion written all over it and he felt bad. She'd been sitting here listening but not able to understand all of it. "I'll fill you in when we're finished here. You can help me piece some things together."

She nodded but said nothing.

Gaige rounded out the discussion. "Okay, everyone at your computers. Let's pull up the records in our files that we have on Caulfield. Comb through those records and look for any mention of buyers, targets, locations, maps, contacts, anything that we can trace back to any one person or organization. I'll contact the police and see what happened to the man captured at the house where Sophie, Dani and Yvette were taken."

The men all moved to disburse, then Gaige stopped them. "One more thing. Tomorrow morning Falcon Montgomery, Ford's son, is coming in for an interview. He's interested in joining us as a team member. We're seeing the change ahead for additional support with Jax and Dodge on baby duty and Sophie and partly me as well. We could use the extra set of hands. And, while we're talking about that. Once Wyatt and Yvette's house next door is completed, I'm shifting some of the scheduling responsibilities to Wyatt. He'll also be backup on covering missions when I'm not available. Any questions?"

Most of them shook their heads, others just got up and moved to a workstation. Lincoln punched Wyatt in the shoulder and nodded.

Axel turned to Bridget, "Let's go upstairs and I'll fill you in on things that transpired. Then we can discuss any ideas you have and if you want to help, we can get you set up to assist us comb through the files for contacts or leads."

"We can stay down here and work if you like." She smiled, maybe a little too broadly and he got the feeling she was enjoying the rush he'd just gotten in gathering intel and the hunt.

"I'd like to see Aidyn, so he knows we didn't take off."

The look she just gave him. The softness in her face, the serene loving feeling he was staring at just now. Wow. He had to hold on to his heart and quick.

35

She'd only been around this group for a day or so but from what she'd seen, they worked well together. Gaige seemed easy to work with and for and the rest of the team seemed strong, capable and smart. They were going to find these jerks. No doubt about it.

She walked with Axel to the elevator and he swiped his key card to open the doors. They stepped in and he pushed "2" to take them up to the sleeping quarters.

Axel looked down at her, after all he was quite a bit taller than she was, so he was usually looking down at her. She enjoyed looking up at him though.

"I'm sorry, Bridget. So much of your life is uprooted or destroyed all at once and I'm sorry for it."

She swallowed because she didn't want to cry. She'd cried enough in the past few days and she was hella proud she hadn't broken down in front of everyone. But now that she and Axel were alone and his compassion and tenderness were directed at her, she was about to lose it. Again.

"I..." Swallowing and breathing in and out a few times, she tried again. "I'll figure it out."

"Well, we have an opportunity, if you will, to make some changes in our lives. I want to be with Aidyn. Close to him, not a weekend dad. I want to be involved. All the time." He seemed frustrated and the elevator doors opened and Sophie and Tate were standing at the doors to get on the elevator.

"Hi, you two."

"Hi, Soph." She looked at Tate's little face, so innocent and pure. "He's just adorable."

Sophie giggled. "Thank you. Of course, we think so. I only hope we can do as good of a job as you've done with Aidyn. He sure is a sweet little guy. He just loves everyone and is so happy all the time."

"Thank you. You'll do a fantastic job as parents. I have no doubt."

She and Axel stepped away from the elevator as the doors closed. She looked up at Axel to see which direction they were going when she noticed his jaw clenched tightly.

"Are you alright?"

His eyes landed on hers. "I'll get used to it, not being part of Aidyn's early life. But it bugs the shit out of me now."

"Oh, I'm sor..."

He held his hand up to stop what she was going to say and shook his head. Apparently he didn't want to hear it.

He walked to the door she and Aidyn and her mom were staying in. Unsure how to proceed he looked down at her. "You want to check and see if he's in there?"

She waved the key card she was given in front of the door and it opened. Quietly peeking inside she looked around and saw her mom and Aidyn coloring at the coffee table in front of the sofa.

Looking back at Axel, she smiled and opened the door wider. Axel stepped in and she was taken by the way he filled the room. Remembering all those years ago why she was so enthralled by him, his movements, his quiet yet commanding presence, goose bumps formed on her arms.

Aidyn looked up and said, "I'm coloring a picture. Wanna see?"

"Sure, honey." Bridget and Axel said at the same time.

A nervous giggle escaped from her and he chuckled. They both walked to the coffee table and sat on the floor across from Aidyn.

Axel smiled at Aidyn, listened to his rambling about his picture and how this purple guy is fighting the orange guy and is going to win. Then his story quickly changed to running somewhere with his red guys right behind and then the story changed again. He had a fantastic imagination. Axel listened to every word. He engaged and asked Aidyn questions while chuckling at his very animated explanation.

It didn't take Aidyn long and he walked around the coffee table and sat on Axel's lap with his coloring book and started showing him his art. Axel gave him his undivided attention and she watched with such pride in her little boy. He really was a sweet happy young man.

Watching Axel interact with him made her heart beat faster. He seemed genuinely interested in everything Aidyn had to say and not just a shallow sort of interest. He wanted to be Aidyn's dad in every sense.

After a little while though he said to Aidyn, "Hey, Bud, we stopped up here to let you know that mom and I have to go downstairs and work for a little while. We're still here in the house, but we'll be downstairs. If you need us, you ask Grandma to text one of us and we'll come and get you for a bit. Okay?"

"Okay. Grandma said we could go outside and play."

"Um..." He looked at her then at her mom. "I don't think that's a great idea, right now. We're in the middle of something but for the time being can you please stay inside?"

Her mom hesitated; her brows furrowed then she looked at her. "Is everything alright?"

"Sure mom, it's all okay. Would you mind taking a walk with me for a minute?"

She glanced at Axel, Aidyn still on his lap, and he nodded at her. She stood and her mom followed her out the door. Walking to the open railing looking down onto the foyer down below and the grand staircase she paused.

"Mom." Swallowing because those damned tears threatened again. "The house and Armed and Dangerous are gone. They were torched today."

"Oh, honey." Her mom's arms wrapped around her and that was it. The flood of tears she'd planned on keeping at bay surged forward and she cried her heart out. Her mom's tears joined hers as they stood consoling each other.

Once she managed to get herself under control she breathed deeply. "We're going to find them and make them pay. But, in the meantime, we'd like you and Aidyn to stay inside. I know he has boundless energy and it's hard being cooped up in this room. You can go down to the kitchen, dining room and living room and walk around the inside of the house. There is a workout room downstairs I'm told. I could see if you and Aidyn could go in there and burn off some energy there."

"Oh, honey, don't worry about us. We'll be fine and we'll stay here inside until we're told otherwise."

"Thanks, Mom. I'll text you in a little while and we'll come and relieve you so you can take a break."

Her mom hugged her again and she swiped at her tears, huffed out a brave breath and started toward the bedroom door when Axel and Aidyn stepped out.

"I just got a text; they have some information. I have to go downstairs. If you want to stay here, there's no problem..."

36

She bit her bottom lip, which was sexy as fuck, but she was working to keep her emotions under control. He could see that her eyes were rimmed with red. She'd likely let herself cry over what had just happened and he felt bad that she needed to act stoic in front of him. He undoubtedly hadn't earned her trust yet.

"I told you I want to be a part of this. I need this."

Then he saw her bottom lip quiver and realized his earlier assessment was incorrect. She was keeping her lip from quivering and from breaking out into a huge cry.

"Okay. I just wanted to offer it up, Bridget."

He turned and knelt in front of Aidyn. "I'll see you later, Bud. Don't forget, if I come back later after you're in bed and you wake up and want to see me, I'll leave my door unlocked. I'm right across the hall, okay?"

"Okay. I'll wake you up in the morning."

"Deal." He put his fist up to bump against Aidyn's and the sharp little tike's smaller fist bumped his. Then the giggle and smile he emitted melted Axel's heart.

He stood and looked at Bridget and Vivian watching them and the smile on both of their faces meant the world to him. They probably didn't even know it. Bridget walked toward them, knelt and hugged Aidyn tightly, her eyes closed as she felt their son's body and tried to absorb him into her. He wanted to do that so bad. Just hold him.

Kissing his cheek, she turned to her mom. "Thank you. Just text if you need a break."

"I will. We're fine. We just might go down to the kitchen and see if Mrs. James has a cookie or two."

"Yay!" Aidyn jumped up and down and Vivian smiled and waved them off.

Axel turned to the elevator and waved his card in front of the electronic pad and the doors immediately opened.

He waited for Bridget to enter in front of him then stepped in and pushed the button for the conference room floor.

"You're good with him."

He turned to her at her words to see if she was teasing him.

"Thank you. I know it sounds trite or too soon, but I love him. I get jealous when you hug him close because I want to hug him to me so badly. But I also want him to want to be hugged by me."

Her phenomenal green eyes turned up to his and his breath caught. The earnestness and depth in the way she looked at him hit him hard.

"I understand that. He's a very loving little boy. I'd bet it won't be long and he'll run to you and throw his little arms around your neck. It's who he is."

All Axel could do was place his hand over his heart and swallow the emotion that just overcame him.

The doors opened and Bridget stepped off the elevator first and he followed quietly behind her allowing himself a moment to gather his emotions and thoughts.

At the conference room door, he reached forward and opened it for Bridget and stepped in behind her. He caught a whiff of her fragrance and it created a riot of emotions warring within him. Maybe working this closely with her was a bad idea. Being in close proximity with her for an extended period was making him yearn for more.

"Here they are." Gaige called out.

Ford and Lincoln came forward to the conference table from a desk in the back of the room with their laptops.

Ford started explaining what they'd found. "We found the connection we were looking for with Caulfield. He was taking women he'd kidnapped to Minneapolis. Jared still had the information we had him search for and we've been combing through it."

Lincoln then continued. "From this information we traced two of the women that Caulfield had abducted and found that from Minneapolis, they were flown to Ukraine and

Poland. We were able to match up their identities with facial recognition at the airports."

"What does this all mean? Axel didn't have the time to tell me more about what happened with Yvette."

Axel turned to her. "I'm sorry. So, Yvette's former boyfriend was using women, in this case Yvette, to keep women at a bar by chatting them up, while he called in a colleague to then come in and kidnap them and sell them. He was running a sex trafficking ring. Once Yvette realized what was happening, she hacked into Caulfield's laptop to find out for sure what he was doing. Caulfield threatened to kill Yvette, so she called her longtime friend, Jax, for help. But, during her time here, Caulfield followed her via her cell phone and found us here as well as Yvette. It's why we don't want Aidyn, or anyone outside right now. If he relayed our location to anyone else, they'll know where to find us. We've got to find them first. That's the short version."

"Holy crap." Bridget then looked at the information before them on Ford and Lincoln's laptops.

Lincoln then added, "We both have security at our homes as well as Jax and Dodge, but regardless, for the time being, the women and children are all coming here. Dodge is managing transport along with Wyatt."

"Where will everyone sleep?" Bridget looked at Gaige.

"We'll sort it out. Mrs. James is working on arrangements for that with Sophie."

"Okay. Aidyn will be happy with more children to play with at least."

She smiled up at him and he couldn't help but smile back. He would be happy to have playmates, even though the only child that was able to play a little bit was Shelby.

"Okay, so back at it." Axel continued. "These women are taken from wherever and flown to Minneapolis and then out of the country? Do we have a location in Minneapolis where we might be able to locate, at a minimum, Victor Book, but ideally, Mikheil Ustymovych or any other known accomplices? Someone else was driving that van that met us on the road the other night."

"Yes, someone was and that was Kash Elliott, an American working with them. It's not confirmed that he took up where Caulfield left off, but he was certainly driving a van with kidnapped women in it. When police got there, he took off on foot, but the van has been taken into police custody and his information was in the van." Gaige responded.

Axel shook his head. "These are either incredibly dumb criminals or they are very arrogant."

Ford stood tall. "I think they're arrogant and feel they are above the law."

Gaige then stood. "I need a team to go to Minneapolis and see if you can locate these guys. We have a general location but nothing definite, though we'll be searching from here."

"I'll go. I want to go." Bridget jumped in.

37

S he quickly formulated her argument should Gaige say no. She wasn't a member of GHOST, but dammit, she wanted to look one of these assholes in the eye as he was being shoved in the back of a police car.

Gaige stared at her for a spit second, then looked at Axel.

"I can keep her close, show her the ropes and work with her. She's a crack shot, very knowledgeable about weapons and obviously is all about safety, so it's not like she's a novice. Former military adds another dimension of depth, too."

Josh walked in the door at that time and said, "I've got some intel on a couple locations in Minneapolis."

"We're sending a team there." Gaige informed him.

"I'm in. Who else is going?"

Gaige looked over at her and Axel. "Josh, here's the rest of your team." Gaige tapped on his laptop. "Wheels up in an hour. All data is uploaded into the server in a separate file in the Caulfield file labeled, 'Ukraine'. Clever, I'm aware." He smirked and she thought he had a dry sense of humor and instantly saw what Sophie had seen in him. Handsome, strong, sure of himself, and no nonsense with an understated wit. That worked.

Axel interjected. "We'll go pack. Josh, we can come up with a plan on the plane."

"Roger that."

Closing his laptop, he smiled and left the room and Axel turned and walked to a desk close to the wall, grabbed a laptop, case and a couple items and tossed them in his laptop case, then walked toward her and nodded.

Without another word they walked from the room, but she heard Gaige say, "Is Falcon ready for tomorrow?"

Trying to keep up with Axel and Josh, who was just stepping on the elevator, she rushed in right in front of Axel. As the doors closed she asked, "How old is Ford's son, Falcon?"

Axel looked over her head to Josh who shrugged. "Mid-twenties I'd guess."

Axel then added a bit more information. "He just got out of the Army after two tours overseas in Afghanistan. Ford shared with him that we're shorthanded now and as we all age out, we'll need new blood, and so encouraged him to come back and work with us. What we do is dangerous, but we have some great equipment and sadly, we're better trained. The military trains the masses, only being able to achieve what their weakest link can achieve. Here, we take that training and enhance it with more one on one training and individualized development."

"Maybe I'll have to apply, too. My livelihood was just torched, and I have all of those skills and then some."

"What about Aidyn?"

She turned to look him in the eye. "Are you going to be less of a father because you have a job?"

"No."

"Why would you think I'd be less of a mother? After all, to this point, I've done it all on my own plus started a thriving business."

"I didn't say you'd be less of a mother. I simply meant, if we're both gone who will take care of him?"

"My mom is here, Axel. She's been taking care of him for us while we're working. She took care of him while I was gone, and you were looking for me. She's been my rock since Aidyn was born."

She tried keeping the sarcasm from her voice but wasn't very successful.

"How would I know that, Bridget? You haven't exactly explained very much to me about how he's been raised. You haven't exp..." His exasperation was apparent. He turned to look straight ahead, his jaw tensing and relaxing as he stared at the elevator doors.

The instant the doors opened she stepped out and he flew past and to his room. Without another word to her or Josh.

Josh stepped off and walked past her and when she opened her mouth to say something, he shook his head and kept walking, but his smirk told her he'd been amused at their argument.

She turned to her room, and luckily hadn't unpacked anything except her shampoo and conditioner. She grabbed those from the bathroom, decided to use the toilet while she was in there, washed her hands and came back out to find her mom sitting on the sofa.

"Hi. Where's Aidyn?"

"In Axel's room. He wanted to bring Axel a cookie from downstairs and knocked on Axel's door. When he opened his door, Aidyn rushed in chatting about the cookie. Axel smiled and waved, and I let them have some time together. They need it you know."

"I know."

"Why didn't you tell me who Aidyn's father was, Bridget?"

It wasn't accusation as much as hurt in her voice.

"I didn't know. Mom. And before you take that the wrong way, Axel was undercover when we met. He gave me a fictitious name. When I found out I was pregnant I tried finding him but, of course, the only person I could find named Robert Beckman was a man in prison. Which, I've now found out was his undercover persona. But, I didn't know his real name and had no way to find him. I never gave him my last name, so he didn't know how to find me."

Her mom nodded as she processed all of this. "Okay. And where does Sophie come into all of this?"

She sat on the edge of the bed, facing her mom. "I was away at a girls' weekend with Sophie, Kate, and three others when I met Axel. They'd all left to go home but my flight didn't leave until the following day."

"Okay." She picked at a thread in her jeans. "What happens now, honey?"

Her shoulders hunched over, and she felt deflated. "I honestly don't know, Mom. Axel wants to be close to Aidyn. I don't have a house or a business to go back to, but it seems like a huge step to move here closer to Axel for those reasons. I could rebuild my business. Even somewhere else. What would you think of that?"

38

Sitting on the floor with Aidyn eating a freshly baked cookie was a pretty great way to spend time with him. He happily chatted about some game he liked which Axel couldn't quite understand and then zoomed right into his friend Rex at school. Which Axel assumed was daycare or preschool. He'd have to ask Bridget. Then the conversation started about a cartoon he loved which featured crime fighting puppies.

Axel asked him questions. "Which puppy is your favorite?" "What does Rex like to do when you play?" Things like that and Aidyn always happily chatted on and on.

He laughed easily and was generally a happy little boy and Axel couldn't have been prouder. Then he stood up and shoved his hand in his pocket and pulled out an action figurine.

Axel stretched his legs out in front of him and leaned his back against his bed and Aidyn quickly climbed on his lap, facing him and pointing to the figurine's special weapons attached to it.

Axel's door opened and Bridget appeared inside, and she quietly came to sit beside him. He was still irritated with her, but it was mostly out of frustration in not knowing and her irritation with her situation. They'd work through it, they had to for Aidyn.

"Hi, Mommy. I'm showing Daddy Megaroars."

Daddy. He called him Daddy. Axel's eyes teared up and he quickly brushed the moisture away.

"Oh, that's a great idea. We'll have to get you some new toys pretty soon. Maybe Daddy will go shopping with us when we do so he can help you pick out the new toys."

Aidyn's eyes locked on his and his smile was huge. "Would you shop with me?"

"Of course. Mommy and I have to go to work for a couple of days but when we come back, we'll go on a big shopping trip."

A couple of things occurred to him right then. He'd spend his whole life savings on this little boy, and he was going to need to find a house and set it up with security, so he'd have a safe place to live with Aidyn when he was with him. Maybe Bridget, too. He'd talk to Ford and see if he was still selling pieces of his mountain since it was largely secured already. Lincoln and Dodge and their families lived at the bottom of the mountain. Or maybe there'd be one of the houses alongside this house that could be persuaded to sell, and he could set up security close to headquarters.

Bridget then told Aidyn, "Honey, Mommy and Daddy have to go to work for a bit. You'll be here with Grandma and you need to listen to her, okay? But when we come back, we'll go shopping."

"Okay."

Aidyn then leaned forward and wrapped his arms around Axel's neck and squeezed him which allowed Axel to wrap his arms around his son and hold him close. Talk about take his heart and make it swell a thousand times. The feelings that little hug stirred in him were enormous. Feeling his little body in his arms, he knew he'd walk through hell for this little human being. His son.

Too soon Aidyn slipped off his lap and jumped to Bridget where she held him close and kissed his head, his ears and then his nose. "I love you, Aidyn. Be good, okay?"

"Love you. I will."

Aidyn stood and looked at Axel, "Love you, Daddy."

"I love you, too, Bud. So much."

His voice cracked and his chest heaved as he watched Aidyn run to the door and pull it open. Bridget stood and followed him out the door and he allowed himself a moment to process what just happened. It was a day he never wanted to forget. Never.

Taking a deep breath, he stood and grabbed his go bag, swiped his eyes, blew his nose, tossed the tissue in the wastebasket and headed out the door. Bridget stepped out of her room at the same time and they walked to the elevator. Then, Josh stepped from his room and Axel smiled and took off running toward the stairs with Josh close behind. Last one ready for a mission had to buy the first drink when the mission was over. No way was he buying.

Luckily he had a slight lead over Josh, but Axel always was faster than Josh. He reached the bottom step and dropped his go bag first and Josh got to the bottom and said, "Shit, I lost last time, too."

They both turned to see Bridget still coming down the steps. Josh laughed. "I'm not last Bridget is. You're buying girl."

"Buying what?"

Axel laughed. "Last one ready for a mission has to buy the first drink once the mission is over. Or breakfast, or whatever is decided."

"I didn't know that." She snipped.

Josh laughed. "Now you do but you're still buying."

Axel said, "You're just happy because it's the first time you haven't lost."

Once she stepped on the bottom step they picked up their bags and headed toward the kitchen. Axel explained, "Mrs. James has little go bags for us with coffees, etc. Let's go stock up before we leave."

They packed up and left the house in Josh's truck for the airport. His heart was filled with so much love and light he felt buoyant.

A text came through from Gaige and Josh tapped the icon on his steering wheel so they could hear it.

"Another woman was reported missing outside the Chicago area. The significance is that this woman is the sister of Kash Elliott. Since he's on the run, the assumption is that they have his sister to keep him quiet."

"Those fuckers need to go down." Bridget snapped from the backseat.

"That they do, Bridget." He responded.

Josh pulled into the airport and parked in the empty hangar, the plane was already outside and ready to go.

He climbed out of the truck, opened the backdoor for Bridget, then walked to the back and pulled their go bags and her suitcase from the back. As Josh locked up, he and Bridget walked to the plane, Gavin was standing outside of the door waiting for them.

"Good evening, Mr. Dunbar. Mr. Vickers has communications for you on the table."

39

Axel had her sitting by the window again as he and Josh went over the paperwork Gavin had from Gaige for them in the plane. She sat quietly as they read, she'd question them incessantly if they didn't share with her what was happening.

Putting her brain in thinking mode she tried comparing her own kidnapping to that of the other women she'd been housed with. They'd each said they'd been drugged. Someone was getting the drugs from somewhere. They'd each been held in one place then transferred to another, and in some cases, to another, so they kept them moving to keep them confused and likely, so no one sent cops in for unusual noises or activity they felt was off.

They had at least two and maybe more transport vans, which meant they had enough people in each city they were operating in to make transportation easy, but that was a lot of trust to ensure all those people were quiet. They probably did just this sort of thing, stole family members or threatened them to keep them honest and working. Honest being used very loosely.

Axel finished reading his communication and handed it to her to read.

"If you have any questions let me know."

She read over the communications and most of which she already knew. The sister of Kash Elliott was 22 years old and taken as she left a night club outside of Chicago. The friend she was with was drugged but left lying on the sidewalk and found by some friends as they left the club. They were trying to get the girl's memory to come back to see if she saw anyone and could identify them.

The general area of Minneapolis that was the hot spot or where their intel was pointing was Carlsford. She wasn't familiar with that area. She'd only been to Minnesota once and that was a long time ago.

There was the information on Caulfield which they'd already gone over and some history on Yvette's incident with him. She read that because she'd only been given the basics of it all. Yvette had been through a lot.

Once she'd finished reading, Axel asked, "Do you have any questions?"

"No, not really, other than how do we proceed from this point?"

Both he and Josh opened their laptops and logged into GHOST to see if there was new intel.

"Holy shit, are you seeing that?" Josh asked.

"Yeah." He looked at her, "It appears that the father of Kash Elliott has called Gaige and offered to pay for the rescue of his daughter and the capture of the men who took her. Apparently Kash is now in protective custody, which doesn't always mean he's safe. They have ways to get to him if they can. Dad's scared and willing to throw money at anyone who can help him. Ford and Wyatt are on their way to the prison to make sure Kash stays alive and we're to continue on to Minneapolis. Apparently, Dad Elliott works in the State Department. Our main contact at the State Department is the one who assigns our government missions and approves and helps us in others. He doesn't even have a code name. Sometimes we get cases from Casper, who's our military contact who reports to the head guy at State. Gaige is trying to get information and assistance from our contact at the State Department."

"Holy crap. What the hell?"

Josh responded. "The Ukrainians could have targeted Kash and lured him with loads of money or power because of daddy's connections. We'll see what that leads to once more intel comes in."

Her mind began to spin.

Axel leaned over as he closed his laptop lid. "You should try and get some sleep, Bridget, once we hit the ground, there will be little time for sleep."

"Okay."

Like she would be able to sleep when this information kept swirling around in her head. She wondered how they did it. Josh moved across the aisle so he could put his feet up and recline his seat, which to the credit of this plane, actually reclined. Just as she thought that, Axel reclined his seat. She looked back at him and he winked at her and smiled. Now her head was spinning in a totally different direction.

He was still the handsome, sexy, powerful man she'd met five years ago. Longer hair, a scar she didn't care about, a couple more lines around his eyes, but his mouth. Oh, the way his mouth made her feel when he kissed her. It was years ago yet she remembered it like it was yesterday.

She must have fallen asleep during some of her thoughts of Axel because the next thing she felt was the plane coming to land. Looking over she noticed Axel and Josh both awake, laptops packed up and ready for action. Clearly this was the life they were used to.

He smiled at her again. "Glad you got a little rest. It might be a few hours before we sleep again."

The plane parked at a private, smaller airport and steps were dropped down for them to disembark. Axel grabbed their luggage from the holding compartment, handed Josh his go bag, then took his go bag and her suitcase down the steps before she could say anything. At the bottom of the steps, he wheeled her suitcase in front of himself and handed it off to her. He didn't stop walking and she figured it didn't do any good to remind him she could have done that herself. Pick your battles as her mom would say.

Once into the airport a manager met them and handed Josh keys to a rental vehicle and they simply strode through to the parking area where a white Tahoe waited for them. Loading their bags into the back, they each climbed in, Josh driving, she in the back and proceeded to drive away from the airport.

"Where are we headed first?" she asked.

Josh was the first to respond as Axel pulled little earpieces from his go bag. "We're headed to a bar on the outskirts of town. Apparently, someone has mentioned seeing a man who looks like Victor Boyko there recently."

"How did you get that intel?" Honestly, how did they get so much information?

"Local PD has been looking and asking. Our contacts have relayed the information."

Glancing at Axel, who didn't seem the least surprised by this, she sat back pondering the reach GHOST actually had and marveling at how no one knew these folks existed and yet look at the information at their disposal.

Axel reached back and handed her two earpieces and an electronic box.

"Put these in your ears and turn the electronic unit on. It keeps us in touch with each other. Try to hide the box, the earpieces are wireless now. We call these our comm units, so when we do a check to make sure we're all on, before we have to separate, make sure you respond so we can all hear each other."

"Okay." She tucked the earpieces in her ears and Axel twisted in his seat. "Are you sure about this?"

"Yes."

"Don't do anything reckless. Don't do anything we aren't all on board with. Do not deviate from the plan."

40

Of course, she was capable, but she was new to this type of work. Also, she hadn't worked with any of them, so this was a risk at best and one he hoped they wouldn't regret.

Pulling two hard covered gun cases from his go bag, Axel pulled out the first pistol, a 9mm, checked the magazine then tucked it in his ankle holster. Doing the same with the second gun in the case, he tucked it in his side holster.

Opening the second case, he checked it as the others, then reached back and handed it to her. "Safety's on, bullet chambered."

"Thanks." Her comment was on the sarcastic side, and he mused she likely didn't need him to check her gun and load it, but he would have done it for...who? Well, none of his teammates since they'd each have their own. Feeling a bit sheepish about treating her as if she didn't know what was going on, he silently admonished himself and made a mental note to remember that she was capable and trustworthy.

He faced forward and worked at getting his head in the game. He wondered how Dodge and Gaige did it when they had someone working with them they cared about and not let that get in the way of what had to be done.

He got a text and pulled his phone up to read it.

"Text from Gaige." He said out loud. "A man fitting the description of Victor Boyko just entered the No Name Bar. He's sitting with two other men at the moment and there seems to be a man patrolling the parking lot."

Josh looked up at his phone in a holder on the dash with the GPS up. "We're five minutes out."

Axel relayed that information via text to Gaige.

"Bridget, did he see you? Will he know you?"

"It's likely that he saw me. He was there in the cabin; I got a stranglehold on him and he passed out. But, it's likely he saw me while I was still under the influence of the drugs."

Axel glanced at Josh. "Okay, here's what we have to do, Bridget, you'll need to duck down and stay in the vehicle..."

"No. I want to be part of this."

Axel huffed out a breath. "If you walk in we blow our chances if he recognizes you. You have to duck down in this vehicle when we pull in the parking lot. Josh and I will go inside. We're connected..." He tapped his ear. "Via our comm units. You can hear what's going on. You'll need to stay as hidden as you can, but still watch their guard in the parking lot to make sure he hasn't made us or if they also wear comm units, that he isn't privately communicating with someone via radio. If you see this, you need to let us know. On the inside, we'll go in and order a drink. We'll get eyes on Boyko and what he's doing. We'll also let you know who he's with via description."

She was quiet so he turned to look at her. Her gorgeous, intelligent eyes stared back at him and he saw her resistance slip away.

"Okay."

She then looked up at Josh in the mirror and he tried not to be irritated at Josh's nod of approval. He only hoped it was to bolster Bridget's resolve to behave and to do what was necessary.

Josh turned on his turn signal. "Up ahead about two hundred feet."

Bridget shrunk down behind the driver's seat and Axel pulled a solar blanket from his go bag and unfolded it. Quickly laying it over Bridget and watching as she made sure she was covered, he turned to face front then turned on his comm unit.

"Comm units on. For now, Boyko is called Number Two."

Josh reached inside of his jacket and clicked his on, then he heard Bridget do the same.

"HQ, comm units on."

"Roger." Came Gaige's reply.

Josh pulled into the parking lot, which wasn't all that large, but large enough. There was a couple dozen cars parked in it that kept them from looking conspicuous.

Spotting a man standing close to the building and watching the cars in the lot, he shared his observation to his teammates.

"Dark-haired man, blue jacket, approximately 5'10". No facial hair, wearing tan kakis and tan loafers. No visible weapon. Current location straight ahead."

Josh nodded and then for Bridget's benefit said, "Roger."

Bridget then responded as well. "Roger."

Josh pulled into a parking spot directly in front of the man, but two rows back and Axel shared that information.

Taking a deep breath, he looked at Josh, "Ready?"

"Yep."

"Bridget, after we leave the vehicle, don't peek up right away. He'll probably be watching us as we walk into the building, but I expect he'll look away shortly afterward. I'll let you know when we reach the door and during our time in the bar, we'll sit so one of us can watch him and keep you updated. If you notice anything out of place, let us know. Here are the keys in case you need them. But, for God's sake, open the doors for us when we come out, especially if we're running."

"Roger."

He glanced at Josh and Josh smirked, then took a deep breath and pulled the keys from the ignition. The nice thing about working with Josh was that he was steady.

Capable, smart and fairly easy going. His half Hispanic heritage was where he and Jax got their olive skin tone, dark brown eyes and deep faith. Their Caucasian father, who had been one of the first GHOST operatives was where they both got their grit, dependability and their love of what they did. It was ingrained in them from the beginning. It had been the same with their older brother, Jake, also an operative, who died like their father on a mission.

He and Josh exited the truck and began walking to the bar, chatting as old buddies do.

"Naw, you're full of it, there's no way the Packers will beat the Vikings, bro." Josh chided.

"You're full of it. How about a wager?"

As they suspected the man outside looked at them, then nodded and looked away, but he was still paying attention to them.

"I'll take that wager. What are you putting up?"

Axel opened the door to the bar and said, "Find us a seat and I'll get us a drink."

Hopefully Bridget understood they were now inside.

He walked to the bar and heard Josh on the comm unit. "Window seat. Looking away."

Axel ordered two beers, which they wouldn't touch, but just the same needed for their cover. Paying for them, he took a beer in each hand and turned and scanned the bar as he walked slightly away from Josh. He acted as if he couldn't see where he was so he could survey a bit more of the bar and its patrons. Finding Boyko in the back corner, he turned direction when Josh raised his hand, playing the game with Axel.

As he walked toward Josh he mumbled in his comm unit, "North corner, white shirt, balding."

Josh nodded since he faced that direction at his window seat.

Axel set the beers on the table and asked, "What did you see?"

"Two men sitting at the table in front of Boyko are his bodyguards inside. They watched you."

Nodding, Axel asked, "Anything outdoors?"

"Yes. We're in trouble."

41

She couldn't believe her eyes. Not long after they walked in the door, the man outside lifted the front of his jacket and she could tell he was speaking into it. He was wearing a wire. He looked in the direction of the truck and she ducked down again. Counting to ten, she peered out between the driver's side window and seat. That's when she saw two guys walking toward the bar, both of them tucking weapons into their waistbands.

"They have comm units. I see two guys walking toward the bar carrying in their waistbands. Both light blonde, six feet tall, one stocky, one thin. Both wearing black pants and tan jackets."

"Roger." Josh responded.

"Shit, two more. Coming from the opposite direction. One of them is very tall, six-four or so. One about five-ten. Just walked in."

She listened to hear if anything happened. Her heart was pounding in her chest and she wondered if this was normal for these guys when they went on missions. You just never knew what might happen.

A tap on the side of the truck caused her to duck down. Then another tap or bump and the vehicle rocked slightly. With the solar blanket over her head, she couldn't see what was happening but the thought that she'd been found out scared the crap out of her. No matter what she'd promised Axel, she was not going to get captured again. Not without emptying her gun into one or more of these bastards.

She waited what seemed like an eternity, not wanting to say anything to Axel and Josh just yet for fear they'd be found out inside.

"Bridget, are you alright?"

Axel sounded worried.

"Yes. Someone is tapping on the truck. I don't know who it is because I'm under the damned blanket." she whispered.

"Two people are making out against the truck. You'll likely feel some rocking pretty soon the way they're going at it."

Josh interrupted. "Company's visiting with Number two."

The Tahoe began rocking and she kept her head low. Vacillating between irritation and interest she wrestled with what to do. She wasn't going to be the one who caused them to be found out.

"Hey, go on and get out of here." A man with a broken accent yelled. She could tell by the sound of his voice that he was coming closer and she held her breath slightly afraid that he'd notice her.

"Fuck off, man." A male said.

"Get out of here you disgusting pigs. What do you say? Get a room."

"Mind your own business, Rusky." A woman said.

"Rusky? You think you're funny? I could kill you and no one would know."

The woman screamed and suddenly there was a fight going on right outside of the SUV. She heard scuffling and the occasional bump against the truck, punches were being thrown, etc. Her curiosity got the better of her.

"What's going on? These two out here are fighting with someone."

"We can see that. Looks like someone took offense to their public display."

"Sheesh."

She gave herself a moment to calm herself and soon the rocking and hitting outside stopped. Slowly lifting her head, she saw a man in his forties walking toward the bar with a woman and the couple that had been making out against the SUV walking toward the back of the parking lot. He was rubbing his face and she dabbed at the other side of his face with a tissue. Rough spot in town.

Josh's voice broke into her voyeurism. "Okay, look alive. Company is leaving."

Slowly turning her head to look out between the driver's seat and window again, she saw the first pair of men she'd spotted leaving the bar.

Then, chills ran the length of her body when she heard in a Ukrainian accent. "What you do here?"

Her heart raced and her breathing came in spurts as she realized they weren't outside the vehicle, but talking to Axel and Josh.

Axel tried being jovial. "Just having a drink, man. Can we buy you one?"

"No. Why you carry weapon?"

Josh chimed in. "We always carry, man. It's a way of life."

"We don't like here."

They were both quiet for a moment. Then Axel said, "No worries, we can just leave."

"Better go now."

Risking a peek at the door Bridget slowly rose from the backseat to peek through her sliver of space by the window. She could hear rustling and movement, but they weren't talking.

The bar door opened, and she watched as the guard turned to watch them, then spoke into his comm unit. As Axel and Josh walked toward the Tahoe, the bodyguard began following them.

"You're being followed by the bodyguard."

The door opened again, and another man walked out of the bar and began following them.

"Another man following you."

Her heart raced and she tried keeping a vigilant watch on them. If they were shot, what would happen? They'd all be killed. Axel turned and glanced briefly at Josh and both men slowed down. She blinked. They slowed down?

Just as the question went through her mind, she saw it happen. The two men following had caught up to Axel and Josh who both swung around and attacked their pursuers. Axel had the bodyguard on the ground and a few well-placed punches had him down for the count.

Josh was just as fast taking the other man out and securing him quickly, Axel and Josh headed for the SUV. Letting out a breath, she dared to relax when all hell broke loose.

42

The bodyguard Axel had left on the ground was on his feet, but Axel quickly spun around and caught the bodyguard by surprise with a solid blow to the jaw. When he stumbled back, Axel took advantage and jumped on him, bringing both of them down followed by a few more brutal blows rendering the bodyguard unconscious.

A quick look over his shoulder and he saw Josh had his guy under control.

"They're coming. Look out."

He turned and saw two men coming from the back of the building pulling weapons from their waistbands. Jumping up he pulled his weapon and ran a good distance around the corner of the building.

Josh followed him around the corner and stopped when Axel did with backs to the wall. Axel took the left side of the wall, and signaled Josh to take the right. As they each crept to their end of the wall, they waited for more men to follow them issuing commands.

A side door on the left, which smelled like it led to the kitchen, had wooden wind barriers on both sides of it. Axel made his way to the first wooden barrier and ducked between the wooden barriers. He whispered into his comm unit.

"Josh, back here between the wooden barriers."

Peeking down each side, he saw Josh rapidly, but quietly, making his way and nothing on his side. When Josh reached him, they found two large dumpsters on the left side of one of the wooden barriers, both in need of emptying by the odors coming from them. And there were several used beer barrels stacked haphazardly against the side of one of the dumpsters.

Taking another look around beyond the side of the building the backdoor opened, surprising them all and out stepped Victor Boyko, escaping out the kitchen door. Classic. Luckily, he was also alone. This meant the rest of the men were on their way around to nab Axel and Josh.

Victor Boyko was as surprised as Axel and Josh, but not fast enough to turn and run back in. Axel grabbed him by the collar and tossed him to the ground and Josh quickly jumped on him and pulled his comm unit from Victor Boyko's waistband. Tucking it in his pocket to analyze later Josh quickly threw a few punches at Victor Boyko and knocked him out, then checked him for weapons. Finding a small handgun, Josh pocketed that as well.

Pushing Victor Boyko against the kitchen door, both men looked around the wooden barriers to see men coming from both sides.

"Here we go." Axel huffed out.

Stepping around one barrier Axel shot the two men coming his way. The element of surprise is always important. Both went down. He turned quickly to see two men coming from the opposite side with their guns raised at Josh. Why wasn't Josh ready? He knocked out Victor Boyko. One was within a couple of steps of them, gun trained at Josh's head.

Just then a horn blaring and the gunning of an engine could be heard, and the two men turned to see the rental vehicle barreling toward them at breakneck speed.

Surprise was replaced with relief when he saw Bridget behind the wheel. She ran the vehicle close to the building and hit the furthest man from the action before he could jump out of the way. His partner took off running but didn't have the speed he needed to get out of the way. Both he and Josh jumped to the side of the building and Axel prayed she'd turn away from them or stop. Otherwise, they'd both be in some serious pain soon.

She turned the steering wheel, just before hitting Josh and slammed on the brakes. The SUV skidded to the side and twisted, hitting the wooden wind barriers, and knocking them over, which also meant they lay on top of Victor Boyko.

"What the hell is going on over there?" Gaige could be heard over their comm units.

"We need local PD. Victor Boyko is down, not dead. We do have the ground littered with bodies though. Not sure how many of them are dead or just out. Gonna need a couple of ambulances, too."

"Local PD is on the way. I called when I heard Bridget say you were being followed out of the bar."

"Roger."

Axel leaned against the SUV to let his heartbeat slow and his mind clear. That was some shit. He looked over at Josh, who leaned against the side of the building doing the same thing and nodded to his teammate, who nodded back. Axel looked down the side of the building where the two men he shot still lay waiting for movement and hoping they didn't move. At least not until PD got here.

The vehicle door opened carefully, and he turned to see Bridget getting out of the driver's seat, her skin pale and her eyes wild.

She stepped down from the SUV and inhaled deeply. Sirens could now be heard racing toward them and he nodded his head. They were going to be alright.

Bridget stood staring at him, unsure what to do and he held his right arm out to her. She raced the couple of steps to him and flung herself into his body, her arms around his waist and squeezed him tightly to her.

He wrapped his arms around her tightly, inhaling the scent of her hair and enjoying the feeling of her body pressed to his. They stood this way for a while, though not long enough, but local PD drove up to each end of the building and barricaded any entry or exit of any other vehicles.

"We have to deal with police now, babe."

She nodded her head, squeezed him once more then stepped back. He looked into her eyes. "You good?"

A faint smile appeared on her lips. "Yeah."

"You did good."

"Thanks. So, did you."

Groaning could be heard from under the caved in wooden barriers and Bridget jumped back and reached for her gun. Axel shook his head no.

"They'll take this. Show them your hands."

Axel turned to face the officers walking toward them, hands in the air. Bridget and Josh did the same.

An officer heard the groaning from under the wooden barriers and Axel filled him in.

"Victor Boyko. He's the man who was involved in the kidnapping and sale of multiple women in the Indianapolis area just a couple of days or so ago and arson among a host of other charges. I'm Axel Dunbar, this is Bridget Barnes and my colleague Josh Masters. We're with GHOST and Gaige Vickers has been in contact with your chief."

The officer called over his radio, "We have a man here believed to be Victor Boyko, injured."

While he waited for a response he looked at Axel, "How many weapons do you have on you, sir?"

They were about to enter into a very long afternoon of questioning and investigation. But it was worth it because they at least had this asshole. Now to get Mikheil Usty-movych. They'd likely not get a lot of information out of Bulikov, he'd likely die before giving anything up. He'd likely die if he did, so he'd be dead either way.

43

There were a few things Bridget knew for certain. She was no shrinking violet by any stretch of the imagination. She served her time in the military, she trained with weapons, hand to hand combat, any number of military machines, including MRAPs and tanks. She excelled and wrapped her arms around any new training and looked for more. She trained other women on the safe, effective handling of firearms and shot them daily. She'd even encountered attacks while deployed in a province outside of Kandahar where she was stationed in Afghanistan. All that, however, was different from what she'd gone through recently. In a matter of a few days, in her own country, she'd been kidnapped and she'd just encountered a shootout to which she'd responded by running a man over with a truck.

All that made her mind spin. But, seeing Axel with a weapon pointed at him and Josh with a gun pointed at his head, that shit was scary.

When she got back to the compound, she hoped Sophie would be up for some girl talk, because she'd like to sit and chat about this stuff with someone who'd been right where she was now. Maybe Yvette would join the conversation, too.

Sitting at the police station for the second time in a week and going over the events that had brought her here today made her weary. She also wondered how these guys did this. All the time.

The officer who'd questioned her earlier entered the interrogation room.

"You're free to go, Ms. Barnes. Your friends are waiting for you in the lobby. Thank you for cooperating with us today."

"You're welcome. Please tell me you have Victor Boyko and you won't let him go anytime soon."

"Yes, we have him in custody and the DA has said he's a flight risk, so they'll likely object to any bail request and the judge likely won't grant it."

"Okay. Thank you."

She stood and the officer opened the door for her and followed her down a hallway. A weird thought occurred to her that all police buildings were mostly similar. Bland in color and decor and unstimulating. She wondered if it were on purpose or due to lack of funding.

Opening the door to the lobby area, she felt relieved when she saw Axel and Josh sitting in the waiting area.

They both stood when they saw her, and as soon as she approached, Josh nodded. "You ready to get out of here?"

"Yes." She softly responded.

Axel stared down at her. "You okay?"

"Yeah. Tired. A little freaked out still and eager to get home to Aidyn."

He smiled, took her hand and began walking toward the door. "Since it's late and we're starving, we thought we'd order in at the hotel so we can shower, then rest up and wait for further information from Gaige. He's been brought up to speed on what happened and has been working with the police to make sure we aren't charged with anything. Sometimes it goes better than others. He may need help from our contact at State. But, for now, we're told to stay put until we're released with no further questions about what happened. Then we're to determine if local PD has, or can get, any intel on where Mikheil Ustymovych is. If he's close, we may have the opportunity to find him."

"What about the man I hit with the truck?"

"He's alive. The last report was that he was seeking extradition to tell everything he knows. Since I doubt the Ukrainians were holding him there on political grounds or some such thing, I expect he'll be allowed to stay here, but it will be in a prison cell."

They climbed back in the vehicle they'd rented. Bridget cringed when she saw the damage to the front of the Tahoe but knew in her heart, it had to be done.

Upon sitting in the back, her body relaxed and she shivered slightly. She fastened her seatbelt and looked over to see her solar blanket still laying on the floor behind the driver's seat. She reached down and pulled it up over her lap, then further up over her shoulders. Axel looked back at her, "Are you feeling alright?"

"Yeah. Likely adrenaline and exhaustion. I'll be fine with a hot shower, some food and sleep."

He nodded his gaze lingered slightly then he turned forward.

Josh spoke up, "I could use about two dozen spicy hot chicken wings."

Axel laughed. "That sounds fantastic."

He turned toward her again. "Bridget, do you like wings?"

"Wings sound great." She turned to look out the window. "And a beer. Or two. I guess I'm buying."

Both men in the front laughed and Axel pulled his phone out and searched for a restaurant close to their hotel. She made a mental note to ask how everything was miraculously done for them. But she knew it was all done from headquarters. Whoever was there watching over their mission, Gaige or someone else, was the one taking care of it all. It made sense since those on the mission had to keep their heads in the game and themselves and anyone on their side alive.

A few minutes later, Josh turned into the parking lot of a hotel, a well-known chain hotel, and she shivered once again. She was one step closer to a shower and a bed.

Pulling their bags from the back of the SUV, she followed behind Josh and Axel as they entered the hotel letting out a breath and relaxing her shoulders. The hotel was warm, inviting and clean. Hat trick right here.

Josh checked them in, and Axel stood alongside her, his arm around her shoulders, which comforted her and almost made her cry it felt so good.

"I'm thankful and proud of you for today, Irish."

Surprised by his use of the nickname he'd given her many years ago, she turned her face up to his. His image waved amongst the tears forming in her eyes. Blinking rapidly to stave off the wave that might follow she swallowed and gathered her emotions.

"I couldn't let them kill you."

"I'm ecstatic to hear that." His comment held the sardonic humor she'd first noticed about him and wave upon wave of memories flooded over her.

Josh turned and tossed a key to Axel. "You two can share a room, I don't want to hear any arguing tonight and I think you have things to discuss. I intend to fill my belly and get some sleep."

He turned and began walking to the elevators and she and Axel followed behind him. He was right. They did need to talk. They needed to talk about a lot of things.

44

A xel offered Bridget the shower first, but she shook her head. "You should go, I want to stand under the water for a long time."

He chuckled. "You got it."

He ducked into the bathroom, taking his go bag with him. He made short work of his shower, opting to not shave, again, he hadn't shaved since he'd found out he had a son. He didn't want Aidyn to be afraid of his face and the scar on it, so he thought if he camouflaged it, it would be less noticeable and therefore less scary.

He dressed in loose gray sweatpants and a darker gray t-shirt, which felt great.

Brushing his teeth, he looked forward to wings and a couple of beers and some time with Bridget. He wanted to know things about Aidyn, about his life and his health and his every day. He wanted to know it all.

He left the bathroom and found Bridget rummaging in her suitcase. She smiled. "Aidyn would love to hear from you. I texted you my mom's phone number so you can call him."

The smile that stretched across his face must have been huge, it felt huge. It also felt thrilling that Aidyn wanted to talk to him. "Thank you."

He sat on his bed, the one without Bridget's suitcase on it, and leaned back against his headboard. Grabbing his phone from his pocket on his sweats, he pulled up Bridget's text, saved her mom's phone number into his contacts, then called Vivian's number to speak to Aidyn.

"Hi, Vivian, it's Axel. I understand Aidyn would like to speak to me."

Vivian laughed. "Oh, he's been so excited to talk to you. Aidyn, it's your daddy."

His heart thumped in his chest. Just hearing that was thrilling.

"Hi, Daddy. Momma said you caught a bad guy today. I'm gonna catch bad guys when I get bigger."

"You are? Well, we'll have to make sure you train good so you can do that."

"Un huh. And today we played in the gym."

"What gym?"

"Sophie made a gym downstairs so I can work out. I have energy Grandma says."

He chuckled. God, he was adorable.

A knock on the door between their room adjoining it to Josh's sounded and he got up and opened the door to the amazing aroma of wings.

Josh's huge grin greeted him along with a beer in his hand for Axel. Josh looked around to hand one to Bridget, but Axel nodded to the shower.

Josh tapped his bottle to Axel's and went back into his room.

"I know you do. Did you have fun working out?"

"I did. I runned. And I jumped really high."

He chuckled and pictured Aidyn's little face as his excitement came over the phone. This little man made life worth living and worth what he did to ensure his young life was filled with all things good.

The phone shuffled a little and Vivian came on giggling. "He just ran off to jump on the bed. I'm afraid he had a piece of cake a while ago and he just got a sugar high. We may go back down to the gym for a while to wear him out."

"So, Sophie created a gym in the house?"

"Yes, down in the workout room because the rubber mats on the floor are safe. She brought in some fun little equipment for the kids, Aidyn and Shelby, to play on to burn up some energy."

"That's wonderful. Where is everyone sleeping?"

"Well, we're still trying to figure that out."

"I'll call Sophie. You and Aidyn should feel free to sleep in my room. Jax can have her room back if she's coming to the house with the babies."

"Thank you, Axel. We sure feel safe here but if we have to leave, we can go to a hotel."

"No. That's not safe at all, Vivian. We'll figure this all out. Thank you for watching Aidyn, hopefully we'll be home tomorrow."

"It's my pleasure. You take care of my girl."

"Will do."

He heard the call end and he quickly typed out a message to Sophie about letting Vivian and Aidyn in his room.

The bathroom door opened, and a fresh, delicious smelling Bridget emerged looking less tired and wrung out than she had when they arrived.

"Food's here if you're still hungry."

"God, I'm starving."

He stood and walked to the adjoining door to Josh's room and opened it. Propping it open with a chair, they walked in and immediately began filling their plates. Axel finished his beer, pulled out one for Bridget and himself. Glancing at Josh, he held up his empty bottle and Axel grabbed another for Josh.

They ate wings, drank beer and chatted about neutral subjects, but it was pleasant.

Bridget began collecting the discarded wings containers, empty bottles and used napkins and set them on the floor by the wastebasket, then turned to Josh and him and said, "Good night."

Axel stood then and nodded to his friend, and walked into their room, closing the door behind him.

Bridget turned to face him, took two steps toward him and leapt up against him, capturing his mouth with hers.

Axel held her close, bending his knees to properly scoop her closer to him, her feet left the ground and she immediately wrapped her legs around his waist. The feel of her body wrapped around his like this was incredible. Especially after what they'd gone through today. Both worried about the other. Both looking out for the other. He'd do whatever it took to keep her and Aidyn safe. Anything.

His hands shifted to cup her ass; the firm globes rounded with her legs wrapped around his waist. He pulled her in closer and her arms tightened around his neck. Their lips played over each other's, his lips fully captured hers. She tasted like beer and wings and she smelled like an angel. Fresh from her shower but as they heated her true scent came through.

His breathing grew ragged and he slowly walked them to his bed. Putting his knee on the bed, he slowly lowered her down then covered her with his body. She wore clothing similar to his, black sweatpants and a dark green t-shirt. She wore a bra under her t-shirt and he admired that she would keep herself covered when Josh was around. He reached up under her t-shirt now, because he wanted to feel her skin, her breasts. He wanted to touch her everywhere.

His fingers found her bra and pushed it up as his fingers kneaded her breast. She arched her back and reached behind to unsnap her bra then she pulled her t-shirt up and over her head, discarding it to the floor. Her bra came next and he couldn't stop looking at her. Faint little marks marred her breasts, where there hadn't been any before. He traced them with his fingers, then kissed them with his lips, admiring her once again for what she'd done to bring their son into the world.

"Do you think they're ugly?" She asked shyly.

"No." His voice was soft, his emotions raw.

Her finger surprisingly traced the scar on the side of his face. "I don't think this is ugly, either."

He swallowed. She lifted herself up while holding his head and kissed his scar. Then she pulled his shirt up to his shoulders and waited for his help in pulling it off.

45

Oh, she wanted him. She wanted him bad. She'd never forgotten him of course and she was mad. And sad. Mostly because she'd so badly misjudged his character. Turns out she had, but in the opposite way she had thought, and it turned out not only was he a good person, he was a friggin' badass.

Seeing him with a gun pointed at him was like a punch in the gut. She couldn't lose him now. They couldn't lose him now. Aidyn deserved to have a father in his life, and he'd taken to him so naturally. To jerk Axel away from Aidyn now would simply be life shattering for Aidyn. And if she were honest, her.

She tugged his shirt over his head and ran her hands over his chest, his arms, his neck, his back. The muscles that bunched and relaxed under her touch were mesmerizing. The fact that he was here with her now seemed like a dream come true. She'd thought about being with him over the years so damned many times. Especially at night.

Damn, the nights were the worst. Especially when Aidyn was a baby, and she was the only parent home with him. She'd put Aidyn to bed and crash in her bed exhausted from keeping up with everything and thinking she'd fall right to sleep, when instead visions of Axel, who was Robert then, danced before her eyes. The way he looked at her when he entered her. The intensity in his eyes when he looked at her. Like he was trying to figure something out but couldn't.

Those hazel eyes, the color his son shared with him, stared at her every day and though she wanted to hate him, she couldn't. Aidyn's eyes would look at her so adoringly and tell her he loved her and his smile, which was a miniature version of Axel's reminded her time and again who Aidyn's father was.

When she found out he wasn't a criminal, he wasn't in jail for going against the law, he was helping people who'd fallen through the cracks. Well, for her, that was like taking an eraser and wiping away all of the bad marks on the chalk board and giving him a clean slate.

"Axel. I don't have a condom."

She hated saying it.

His smile grew, and his eyes stared into hers for a long time. He kissed her lips softly, then said, "I might."

He got up and went to his go bag on the floor alongside his bed and pulled out the jeans he'd worn today. Then snagged his wallet from the back pocket and opened it up.

"I have this one, but it's about 5 years old."

She lifted herself up on her elbows. "What?"

He showed her the worn package the condom was in and shrugged. "I haven't been with anyone since you."

Her eyes grew large as she stared at him. "Really?"

"Yeah."

She sat up. "Why?"

He came and sat next to her on the bed. His head shook slowly.

"No one appealed to me anymore."

His cheeks tinted pink and her eyes teared up. "Me, either." She said softly.

"Really?"

She scoffed slightly. "Well, I was a single mom with a newborn and trying to open a business at the same time. I was either exhausted or crabby or broke."

She turned to look at him. "And, no one appealed to me, either."

He leaned into her, his right arm wrapped around her and his hand held her nape as he kissed her. His lips softly covered hers. Then they moved so their lips danced the most glorious dance, soft one second, demanding the next. Warm, wet and eager to taste the other fully. To feel and show their feelings the next. It was The. Best. Kiss. Ever. It said everything words couldn't say.

He lay back and pulled her down on top of him. The feel of their naked torsos against each other was electric. His torso was firm and muscular where hers was soft, her breasts pressed into his firmness was such an exquisite sensation.

His thumbs then hooked into her sweats and panties and began tugging them down over her hips and she lifted herself up to aid him.

His cock thickened between them and as she lay on him, the feeling of his hardness against her clit was exhilarating. Oh, it had been so long since a man, this man, had touched her. She'd almost forgotten the feel of him. She even worried over time that what she remembered was exaggerated in many ways in her mind. It wasn't.

Once her sweats were to her knees, she lifted one leg out then shook her pants off the other leg, freeing her body to then straddle his.

She rubbed herself against him and closed her eyes at the friction. The feeling was like a little bit of heaven and a little bit of hell.

Lifting herself up on her knees, she began pulling at his sweats thrilled that he eagerly helped her.

"Are we going to risk using this?"

"Yes."

She continued helping him remove his pants, as sexy as he looked in them, he looked so much better without them. When he came into view, his long, thick length, so ready for her, her breath caught. He was simply perfection.

She lay fully on top of him, her body moving, mimicking the dance they would soon fully engage in. His hips rose and fell in time with hers as their lips devoured each other. His breathing was ragged, his body heated and the warmth created from their movements was invigorating.

He reached for the condom he'd laid on the bed and ripped the package open. She took it from him, then sat up on her knees still straddling him. His rigid length was impressive between her legs. She couldn't wait to feel him inside of her. Laying the condom on top of the head of his penis, she slowly rolled it over him, adding pressure and her hand moved lower and lower, then slid back up to swipe her thumb over the head and then back down. His cock jerked, his nostrils flared and the look in his eyes when she looked up at him was hot. Inferno hot.

She smiled, then slowly rose above him. Using her left hand to position him at her entrance she could feel his strength as he held himself back. He was wild right now. Ready to go like a stallion in the paddock waiting to go win a race. But he controlled himself.

Slowly, she slid down on him and both of them moaned. Oh, the feeling. His firmness filled her until she rested fully on top of him. She looked into his eyes and halted for the briefest of moments, both of them memorizing this moment in time. Leaning forward, she kissed his lips, softly, swiping across them with her tongue which elicited a groan from him. Nipping his bottom lip, she rose up slightly, her hands on either shoulder, and seductively began riding him. Even strokes up and down brought them both pleasure. Immeasurable pleasure. Feeling him inside of her once again, it was rejuvenating. Like all the hurts of the past failed to exist right now. Her body accepted him inside like he was made for her.

Plunging down on him again and again she felt her orgasm rolling toward its end faster than she wanted. Her body moved faster than she wanted but she was unable to stop it. Falling down on him, she groaned into his neck as she reached her orgasm then sighed as it seemed to continue pulsing through her.

His arms circled her back, pulled her tightly to him, then faster and more graceful than she'd ever have imagined, he rolled them over, so she lay under him, and he started the movements once again, in and out of her, in and out. Her hips rose to allow him to fully seat inside of her and she moaned when it felt as if he were deeper in her than before. Her legs rose and wrapped around his back and he slid in once again, deeper still and her breath caught. It was as if that just lit a flame and she was soon eager for another orgasm.

Their movements were fluid and in sync and the look in his eyes, that same look that made her feel as if he were trying to figure something out, pierced her. She was unable to look away from him as he brought her once again to a broiling, hot orgasm then he quickly allowed himself a release, his groan sounded in her ear and his ragged breathing continued through his orgasm. His left hand quickly slid to the side of her face and he held the side of her head and his lips pushed in tightly to her neck and kissed her gently.

"You are my heart, Irish."

A single tear slid down her temple as she lay there listening to their breathing and felt his body weight on her. It was the best feeling. She'd missed him so much, which seemed weird because they'd only known each other one night. One, very busy, very sexual night. The one and only time she'd had a one-night stand.

46

She sniffed. He lifted his head to look into her eyes. "Are you alright?"

She nodded and he saw the wet trail the tear had made down her left temple. He swiped it dry with his thumb but looked into her eyes. His brows furrowed and she lifted her left hand to softly massage the space between his eyes.

"You've looked at me like this before. Like you're trying to figure something out. Do I remind you of someone?"

"No. You are like no one I've ever known."

"Then what are you trying to figure out?"

He grinned, then his handsome face took on a serious look once again.

"I can't figure out why it feels like we're supposed to be together. When I first met you, it was as if the universe was telling me you were mine. We were supposed to be a couple. I can't explain the feeling. I've never had it before."

Her hand floated into his hair and pulled it away from his face. Mimicking the motion with her other hand, she looked him square in the eyes and what he saw reflected back at him was overwhelming. It wasn't disgust at the scar on his face, or anger for the years they'd been apart and she raised their amazing son alone. It felt like love.

She pulled his head down so their lips touched and the softness of her lips against his was thrilling. They were such a contrast to each other. She was softness and curves where he was firmness and bulk. Her skin was flawless and soft while he was flawed.

Yet, when he looked at Bridget, she was perfection.

He pulled himself from her, reached for a tissue and discarded the condom.

Bridget scooted up the bed and slid under the blankets and he did the same, pulling her quickly into his arms. He hung onto her like she'd slip away. His heartbeat increased when she wrapped her arms around him and pulled him close.

He didn't remember much more before sleep took him. He actually woke up a few hours later, the lights still on but Bridget sleeping deeply alongside him, and he couldn't remember feeling more satisfied with his lot in life as he did right then.

***

The ringing of his phone woke him, by the time on the face of it, two hours later. GH, GHOST Headquarters, name on the readout woke him instantly.

"Dunbar."

"Axel, Gaige. We have a line on Ustymovych. He's enroute to Minneapolis via a private plane. We had Jared Timm do a bit of research for us and he was able to hack into a phone number we found on the cell phone from Viktor Boyko, the dead man at the cabin, where Bridget and the other women were found. Jared traced the phone number to see where he is and has just confirmed it's in fact, Ustymovych."

"Okay. Do you want us to follow him?"

"Local PD has been called. But, we've discussed this with them, and they are afraid if they go in with unis, he'll run. So, you and Josh need to get there before Ustymovych. Plant yourselves at the gate where his plane will arrive. Then follow him to the vehicle picking him up. Once he's at the vehicle, local PD will arrest him, but we want him out of the airport. We also have reason to believe accomplices will be there to receive him. We want them all."

"Roger." He looked over at Bridget, who was wide awake and sitting up next to him. "What about Bridget?"

"Is she up for this?"

Bridget nodded and he grinned. "She says yes."

"Then, the same rules apply to her. The airport will let you carry inside. Since it's a private airport, off the main airport's property, but still on the grounds, we've cleared this. That's the other reason they want him apprehended outside. They don't want their place shot up."

"Roger."

"One last thing. Authorities want him alive. But, they said if he can't be brought in alive, dead will do. They don't want him in the wind."

"Roger that."

The line went dead, and Axel looked into Bridget's eyes. "Did you hear all of that?"

"Most of it."

He kissed her lips. "Gotta hustle, Irish."

"Roger."

She grinned but scampered off the bed, though not before he was able to swat her ass and enjoy the red mark as it formed on her skin as she walked to the bathroom.

He quickly dressed and once Bridget left the bathroom, he quickly used the toilet, washed his hands, brushed his teeth and opened the adjoining door to Josh's room.

Josh was dressed and packing things into his go bag.

"Gaige called, bro. I'm ready."

Axel nodded then went back into his room with Bridget and began packing up their belongings.

Bridget was packed much faster than he imagined and when he looked at her and smirked she retorted. "Army strong, baby. I've had to move out fast before."

He nodded, hefted his bag over his shoulder and opened the door to the room, waiting for Bridget to exit before him. Time to go get this piece of shit so he could go home and play with Aidyn.

After checking out they loaded up the SUV. The dents and dings looked far worse today than they did yesterday. Good thing GHOST always insured their rental vehicles. They usually came back a bit worn and abused.

He opened the backdoor for Bridget and she climbed in with a wink. The sultry little vixen wore a pair of jeans, which fit her perfectly, and a white t-shirt, which made his cock tingle a bit. Now that he'd had her again, he'd have a hard time not dreaming about the next time, which hopefully would happen soon.

He climbed in the front seat and as Josh drove, he began working to distribute the comm units and prepare for what lay ahead. Which hopefully would be a smooth apprehension. At least he could hope for that.

47

Today she was ready. Yesterday had been a hell of a ride. Partly because Axel felt strongly about shielding her from being taken again and, rightfully so, she wasn't part of the official GHOST team. In all honesty, she didn't really want to be, either. Not fully. But this mission was personal. She and Aidyn needed to know with certainty that they weren't going to be hunted again. 'Cause, honest to God and anyone else listening, she could and would, kill anyone trying to take her son. Without hesitation.

The other part of yesterday had thrown her back into a pseudo-war zone without much thought as to what she was getting into. Her Army days were behind her and she'd never dreamed she'd be back there again. But, today, after processing yesterday and reconnecting in the most delicious way with Axel, she was ready.

Axel looked back at her and handed her a comm unit.

"You ready for today?"

"Yep. Never been more ready."

"Okay. Should I be worried?"

She chuckled. "Not unless you plan on trying to stop me from doing what needs to be done."

Josh laughed. "Whoa, Axel, you've got your hands full."

Bridget caught Josh's eyes in the mirror. "No one has their hands full of me unless I decide it to be."

Josh simply replied, "Noted." But he smiled and wisely continued watching the road.

Axel chuckled but said nothing, which Bridget took as a good sign.

She tucked her comm unit into her waistband and untucked her t-shirt so it was covered. Inserting an earpiece into each ear, she pulled her hair forward over her ears and felt ready.

Axel twisted in his seat. "So, we'll go in separately but stand close to the gate. I'll text you the gate and his picture. Once anyone has eyes on him, we relay that information to the others. HQ will be listening to everything as well. Remain inconspicuous. We need to follow him, so again the first to see him, relay that information until the next one has eyes on him. That person will follow for a while until the next has eyes on him. Once he leaves the airport terminal and heads to a vehicle, we'll basically be backup for local PD. If he runs, we can give chase if necessary, but take our cues from PD. Questions?"

"No." She was already pumping with adrenaline.

Josh asked. "What if he isn't alone?"

"We'll keep everyone informed. Stay back and don't put yourself in danger. If they get in their vehicle, we're screwed because we don't have a vehicle to give chase, so we can't let them get to the vehicle."

"Roger."

She ran it all through her mind again then asked, "Did they find all the women?"

Axel shrugged then dialed his phone.

"HQ - Lawson."

"Hey Wyatt, Bridget is asking if the other women were all recovered from where these guys had them."

"All have been recovered that haven't been sold off. We are still tracking where he flies them once they leave the US. Right now, it's looking like the trail is leading to the Middle East."

"Oh, God." She sighed. "How horrible. Women are treated like shit there."

"Agreed." Wyatt responded. "We're doing what we can to try and find them. Jared was able to tap into a computer system through Caulfield's computer information we have here. He's managed to get us several contacts, buyers and resellers in other countries. We're tracking them all down the best we can. We're also trying to get clearance through Casper, to get over there and find them ourselves. So far, the military has teams over there and they are trying to do what they can on their end. But, we won't just leave them to die there. We'll do what we can."

Axel looked back at her and nodded his head. "Thanks, Wyatt. Where's Gaige?"

"So, Gaige, Sophie and Tate flew out to California to Camp Pendleton. His niece, Emersyn was wounded in a skirmish in Afghanistan. They flew her back to Cali and they are meeting Dane and Keirnan there to see Emmy."

"Shit," Axel swore. "She going to be okay?"

"We don't know anything yet."

She sat back into the seat hard. Sending up a prayer for Emmy, then another prayer that they stopped this bastard. Not that he'd give them a ton of information, but they'd at least stop this leg of the sex trafficking ring and maybe really put a dent in it. With great luck, they'd actually be able to recover some of the women.

Josh turned the SUV into the airport driveway, turned right and led them to a smaller airport to the right and behind the main airport. The smaller airport for private planes, where business executives, rich playboys and those who didn't want to deal with common folks played. She'd been around a few of these airports in her day when she worked for a catering company.

She sat forward. "Does he take the women out in these types of airports? For instance, is there an employee or two here who help him load these women up after hours and fly them out of here? Where is he taking these women from, landing, and loading them?"

Josh looked up at her in the mirror then over at Axel.

Axel replied. "That's a great question. Wyatt, you have anything on that?"

"Working on it. Initially one of the captives from the cabin mentioned a little airstrip out in the middle of nowhere in Minnesota, but we called local PD and they took a look. There was nothing there but field planted with corn. No way to land a plane there."

Axel responded, "It would make sense to change their location around so no one could double-cross them or rat them out if the locations each time were secret. Also, when this plane drops him off, what are the chances that we could take a look inside and make sure he isn't having women loaded into that plane while he's here. He could be a red herring for us to follow him while the nefarious acts are going unnoticed."

"Great point, Axel. Let me check with local PD and see if someone can get inside that plane. Not sure if it's rented or owned by him. Warrants will need to be granted. Maybe."

Wyatt chuckled lightly but she got the drift. If they could squeeze between the lines they would. Josh turned the SUV around and backed in alongside the building.

Wyatt came over their comm unit once more. "Gavin is arriving with the GHOST plane in about fifteen minutes to bring assistance and you back once this goes down. It's also great cover for you all."

"Roger." Josh responded.

A male walked up to the side of the Tahoe. He wore a white and gray loose-fitting shirt over khaki's and white tennis shoes.

Rolling down his window the man said, "Private property."

"We're supposed to pick up a package for Mikheil Usty-movych." Josh replied.

The man looked at each of them through the vehicle window then said, "Wait."

He stepped away from the SUV, pulled a cell phone from his pocket, and began talking to someone. He turned to watch them as he had his private discussion and her pulse raced faster than the engine of a plane taking flight.

"Yeah. Go in." The man waved toward the door.

For good measure, Bridget exited from the opposite side of the vehicle as him. Axel ushered her inside and they made their way to the back of the airport and where the runways were. There weren't a lot of people around so blending in would be a bit tricky. She found a woman sitting in a chair near Gate A, which is where she and Axel were to be positioned and sat one seat away. As soon as she sat down, a man came from across the room and sat on the opposite side of the woman and Bridget noticed that she visibly stiffened.

Axel situated himself outside of Gate A. From where she sat, she couldn't see him, but his whisper in her ear, "Set." told her he was there. Josh stationed himself at Gate B, and as soon as Gate A disembarked, Josh would be the first to follow Ustymovych until he was in Axel's sight. Bridget was to keep an eye on Ustymovych to make sure he actually left via the main exit, but if not, she needed to have eyes on him until Axel and Josh could get in place.

The woman next to her moved her arm slowly to lay it on the seat between them and Bridget looked over at her. She stared straight ahead but her fingers, still laying on the empty seat curved up and down as if seeking assistance.

48

Axel stood just outside of Gate A, assessing the area for any doors that could lead to somewhere else and any spaces where one could duck out without being seen. He took the stance of looking nonchalant, as if he were waiting for his plane to arrive.

An employee approached him, and the tall slender man dressed in black slacks, black shoes and a crisp white shirt with a black tie nodded at him. "Sir, is there anything I can offer you while you wait?"

"No thanks, it shouldn't be much longer."

The tall man nodded then stepped back a step before turning to walk into the Gate area. He listened as the same man walked to the passengers waiting in Gate A.

"Ma'am, is there anything I can get for you while you wait for your plane?"

Bridget's voice, so sure and clear, "No, thank you."

The man then moved to another passenger and asked him something to which the man responded in a terse voice, "She isn't feeling well. We don't need anything."

Bridget's voice again. "Is there anything I can do for you? I may have something for your tummy if you need it."

The strange man's voice repeated, "No, she doesn't need anything."

Axel stepped into the Gate A area to get a visual on Bridget. She sat with one chair between her and another woman, the woman's hand lay in the empty seat between them and Bridget turned in her seat to look at the woman.

The man on the other side glared at Bridget, likely warning her to back off and she instantly knew this woman was likely a captive, drugged to keep her docile.

"My name is Bridget." She held her hand out for the woman to shake her hand. The woman slowly lifted her hand, but her coordination was shaky.

"Angel." Her words were slightly slurred.

"I'm sorry. I didn't quite hear you." Bridget said.

Axel's heart began racing, she was good, but putting herself in danger.

Keeping his voice soft, he asked, "Wyatt, did you hear that?"

"Yes."

"She said her name was Angela. Now please, leave us alone." The man sitting next to Angel said.

Bridget looked over her shoulder to see Axel watching her.

He slowly shook his head no. They'd try to save this woman, but they had to get Ustymovych first. His gut told him that Bridget was already thinking along other lines and there was little he could do right now, without blowing their cover to stop her.

"Wyatt's voice whispered over the comm units. "Angel Elliott. Kash Elliott's sister."

A plane landed just beyond the building and Axel watched from his vantage point as it slowed, then began its taxi to their Gate.

"We have a landing." He told his colleagues.

He glanced at Bridget again and saw that she reached over and held the hand of the woman in the seat. Angel Elliott.

Wyatt then spoke, "Gavin just landed."

Glancing out the windows, he saw the GHOST plane land and slow on the runway. Perfect timing and great cover.

The GHOST plane taxied just outside of the Gate, behind the plane Ustymovych was likely on, and cleverly parked Ustymovych's plane in. The man with Angel Elliott became agitated further and looked over his shoulder to a man who had appeared from a hidden doorway. Axel watched the door close, and quietly said, "Hidden door in the wall, disguised by trim work. No handle visible. East wall."

Josh responded, "Roger."

The man that appeared seemed younger in appearance, likely in his early twenties, dressed much like the manager had been dressed. Axel looked around for the manager and wondered where he'd gone.

"Manager missing. The man who came out of the hidden door was dressed like a manager. He may be taking the missing manager's place."

Bridget's head followed the younger man as he walked out to the GHOST plane and began signaling for Gavin to move the plane away from Ustymovych's.

Gavin acted unable to hear, and actually shut the plane off and as slowly as he could, lowered the airstrips that allowed passengers to board and alight. After what seemed a very long time, Gavin appeared in his usual impeccable uniform.

The man stood before Gavin, arms flailing around wildly, his raised voice able to be heard inside the airport, though not the exact words. Axel watched as Gavin looked at the man as disinterested as he could, then nodded and went back to the GHOST plane.

The airstair to Ustymovych's plane lowered and two men slowly descended the stairs, looking around carefully and suspiciously.

Axel reported. "Looks like two bodyguards."

Wyatt responded. "We've got two more on our plane, too."

Ford and Lincoln began their exit from the GHOST plane, looking for all intents and purposes, the wealthy businessmen this airport catered to. Each of them carried small bags which could be considered nothing more than an overnight bag, but Axel knew from previous experience, were likely loaded with support gear. They were also heavily armed.

Feeling better about the support, he glanced once again at Bridget, who stood as if she were eager to greet a lover or a friend. She looked down at Angel Elliott, who had managed to lift her head and look up at Bridget. Bridget's only movement was a very slight nod. She then looked up at him and his heart raced. He knew what she was going to do.

Softly talking into his comm unit he said, "Irish, you be careful. If you can, get her to the GHOST plane."

"Yes."

Ford looked into the window of the airport, which was one way glass, but he let them know he could hear, then he cocked his head toward the agitated manager letting them know he had that one.

Lincoln chuckled but said nothing.

The man sitting with Angel stood watching the players in action. Axel stood tall, "Josh, get ready."

"Roger."

Ustymovych began to descend the airstairs looking smug, confident and arrogant. The sun gleamed off his bald head. The sunglasses he wore shielded his eyes from more than the sun; they prevented any onlookers from seeing where he was looking. The two bodyguards who'd disembarked earlier, each stood at the bottom of the steps looking around for any signs of anything unusual or out of place. Ustymovych was expecting trouble.

"Two at the bottom of the steps, one hassling Gavin, one in here that I can see." Axel relayed to his team.

As the man with Angel took her by the arm and helped her stand up, Bridget looked at the door, her eyes on Ford and Lincoln. The man jerked Angel to brush past Bridget, but Bridget stepped in front of them.

"Oops, sorry. I'm just so excited to see my boyfriend."

She basically blocked their exit to the door and as Lincoln opened the door she ran to him and hugged him.

"That is Angel Elliott with that asshole coming this way."

Lincoln hugged her with one arm and spun her around, blocking the door. As the door opened and Ford walked in he pushed them further into the room.

"Get out of our way." The man bitched.

Ford stepped forward. "Sorry old man, but my buddy here missed his little lady." He looked at Angel then back at the man. "You must know how it is."

Ustymovych then walked in the door and was caught up in the throng of bodies. While his bodyguards were trying to move him past Lincoln and Bridget, Ford somehow managed to maneuver himself between one of the body-guards and Ustymovych. Lincoln then let go of Bridget, which relieved Axel, and stepped in between Ustymovych and the other guard and there seemed to be a plethora of people all vying for some semblance of position.

The man ushering Angel through finally managed to get them untangled from the throng of people and opened the door to walk out to the plane. Bridget turned to follow them as did Ford.

49

The oddest thing about all of this was that she didn't feel scared, not for herself, but for Angel. Feeling emboldened knowing Ford was behind her she looked at him, and when he nodded, she pushed between Angel and the man. She grabbed Angel's arm and began to run with her.

"I know you've been drugged, but if there is anything you can do to help me, I sure could use it now."

Angel stumbled along as she heard Ford land a couple fierce punches on the face of the man who'd been holding Angel. The younger man who was watching the plane and trying to get Gavin to move turned to see her running the best she could toward the GHOST plane. She saw as soon as he realized what was happening.

He began running toward them and Bridget pulled her weapon. He froze, then reached for his weapon but not before a shot rang out from above. Looking up Bridget felt relief surge through her when she saw Gavin with a gun.

Somehow Gavin had managed to get away from the younger man and reached the plane before Bridget and Angel did. They ran toward the plane, Angel stumbling along but it was as if the adrenaline surge began to help her metabolize the drug.

Bridget holstered her gun and pulled Angel to the steps, got her up two steps then began pushing her to get going faster. At the top of the steps, Gavin reached out and pulled Angel inside and Bridget quickly followed.

"We're in the plane." She said to the GHOST operatives.

Her breathing came in short spurts, but she was so relieved. Gavin had two bottles of water out of a cooler and opened them for Angel and Bridget, who smiled. "Thank you so much for the cover."

"All in a day's work." he retorted.

"Can you watch that she's alright? I have to go back and assist them."

Axel's voice came on the comm unit. "Nice job, Irish."

Through her comm unit she could hear various scuffles and fighting as her "teammates" worked their way through the throng of Ukrainians. Remembering where the SUV was parked, Bridget nodded to Gavin, turned to Angel and said, "Stay with him. We'll get you back home."

Angel nodded, some of the color coming back to her pretty face.

Bridget quickly descended the airstairs and ran around the building in the direction of the vehicle.

The run felt good; she'd not had the chance to run in the past few days. The sun was out and visibility was great.

Josh asked, "Bridget, where are you?"

"Running to the SUV."

"Keys under the seat."

She smiled and if she had to run over one or two more of these fuckers, so be it. A gunshot sounded then another and she slowed her running.

No one said anything for a few seconds and her pulse raced and she felt sick.

"Axel?"

He didn't say anything, and she picked up the pace. No, this couldn't happen now.

"Irish, I'm okay." He sounded pained but alive.

She rounded the first corner and saw the truck up ahead. Mustering all of her energy, she pushed forward as fast as her feet would take her.

Lincoln's voice sounded next. "PD has him."

Josh sounded winded. "Confirmed."

Wyatt then came on. "Roll call."

"Josh."

"Ford."

"Lincoln."

"Bridget."

Finally, "Axel."

A sob broke from her throat. She made it to the SUV and jumped inside. Driving around to the front of the building she saw Axel laying on the ground, Josh not far from him. Lincoln and Ford were huffing against the building. Usty-movych was handcuffed and being shoved into the back of a police car. In two other police cars, his comrades were already sitting in the backseats looking a tad bloodied and the worse for wear.

She stopped the truck and put it in park. Jumping out she ran to Axel, who was beginning to sit up on the ground.

"Are you alright?"

"Yeah." His voice was tight, and it looked like it hurt to breathe.

"Are you shot?" She looked around for blood but couldn't see anything.

"No." His breathing was ragged, and he leaned forward.

Josh finally said, "He got kicked in the nuts."

Ford and Lincoln chuckled slightly, though when she looked at them they both grimaced.

"Which fucker did that, I'll go kick him in the nuts for trying to ruin my fun."

This got the men laughing, including Axel, sort of, who then coughed, then groaned.

As soon as they were all able to catch their breath, Wyatt got them moving.

"Wheels up in ten minutes."

Bridget reached down to help Axel stand up. Upon standing, he heaved out a big sigh, "Damn that hurt."

"You looked like you were in a fair amount of pain."

"Jesus."

They hobbled back to the building and the sight of the vehicle caught her attention.

"Do I need to move the SUV?"

"No, I've got someone from the rental agency on their way to pick it up. How bad is it?" Wyatt asked.

She bit her lip, "On a scale of one to ten, I'd give it a four."

Wyatt responded, "That's not bad. It's usually worse."

Walking through the airport, and to the backdoor she saw police officers around Ustymovych's plane and one police officer walking down the airstairs of the GHOST plane.

The officer met them on the ground and stopped to talk to Josh.

"She wants to go back with you. Her parents have been called and they'll make arrangements with you to get her back. She's scared and trying to work through the drugs right now."

"Thank you, Officer."

The young officer nodded and waved at each of them as he walked to his fellow officers to continue processing Ustymovych's plane.

All in all, Bridget felt pretty good about how things went down today, but it also solidified in her mind that she much rather preferred teaching women how to defend themselves than actually working in the field as the GHOST team did. But it was gratifying, and she could see the appeal.

She'd keep pushing for information on whether they'd found the women who'd been stolen and sold like cattle previously, though it seemed like trying to find a needle in a haystack and send prayers for their safety. But each of these women had families and hopefully these families would continue to keep pressure on the local, state and federal government to help find them.

She slowly climbed the steps to the plane, and once on board she sat next to Angel, and held her hand for reassurance. Axel sat across from her and Josh across from Angel.

Ford and Lincoln sat across the aisle. They buckled up and prepared to take off.

"Comm units off during takeoff folks." Gavin's voice sounded over the intercom.

Bridget immediately turned her comm unit off, pulled out her earpieces and lay them on the table between her and Axel.

She caught his eye. He smiled. It was a brilliant smile, his face, though a bit battered from a fist fight, the face she'd dreamed about so damned many times in her life made her smile in return. He winked at her and her smile grew.

Now, she just had to figure out what to do about her house and her business and where they went from here.

50

Axel woke with his son snuggled into his side, his precious little face so peaceful and innocent in sleep. His tousled hair brought a smile to Axel's face. Every time he looked at Aidyn he just wanted to say, "Wow."

Looking across the bed, lay Bridget, her hands folded together and tucked under her cheek her long lashes resting on her cheeks and her gleaming red hair soft and fanned around her.

They'd all doubled up while everyone was back at the compound until the Ukrainians were captured. They were still waiting for confirmation that there weren't any lose ends before they all resumed their normal lives. Which brought him around to what a normal life would be for him from this point forward. He had no intention of staying here while Bridget and Aidyn moved back to Stueben. He wanted them to be with him. Knowing that he and Bridget still had things to work out and to be honest, they needed to spend some time getting to know each other, but he already knew she was the one for him. Hadn't the last five years of abstinence proved that no one else appealed to him but her?

He got up gently so he didn't wake them and noticed that Vivian was not on the sofa where she'd fallen asleep last night. Checking the bathroom, he surmised that she'd gone down for coffee. He glanced at the clock on his bedside table to see that it was 7:15 am.

Entering and closing the bathroom door, he used the toilet then turned on the shower. Undressing he stepped under the hot water and let it pummel down on his battered body. Soaping up and washing himself he then washed his hair and stepped under the hot water to rinse off.

Soft warm hands slid up his sides as full firm breasts pressed themselves into his chest. His left arm wrapped around her body, and together they took a step from under the spray of water. Wiping the water from his eyes, he looked down into her face. Water dotted her cheeks as it splattered on her but then her mouth captured one of his nipples and sucked it into her warm wet mouth.

His cock roared to life which she immediately noticed and reached for. Her hands pumping him as the warmth of the shower and the water sliding over their bodies was about the sexiest thing a man could imagine. She continued to pump his length with her hand as his hands explored her body. She was fine, so very fine.

He ran his fingers firmly up the seam of her ass and her breath caught. She turned quickly and planted her hands against the back wall.

"If I recall correctly, you said you liked it doggy style the best. No, wait, you said it was your favorite position." she purred.

His eyes devoured her body, the water sliding over her creamy round ass and her body opened for him.

Positioning his cock at her entrance he entered her slowly, then pulled out, watching as her body once again accepted him inside. The feeling of the water and her body warmth mixed together and watching his cock disappear into her body was fucking sexy.

Pumping in and out of her several times, the feeling like no other, his balls began to painfully draw up as the tightness in his cock threatened to explode, he pulled out of her and spun her around.

"That used to be my favorite position. Don't get me wrong, it's fucking sexy. But my new favorite position is facing you, looking into your eyes as I'm in you. Watching your face when you let go and your orgasm takes over. Man, I'll never get enough of that, Irish."

He pressed her back to the wall of the shower, bent down to hook her left leg over his right arm, positioned his cock at her entrance and tilted his hips as he entered her. She moaned softly, her hands hanging on to his shoulders as he continued to pump into her over and over again. His balls once again tightened, and he rotated his hips to hit her clit.

"Irish..." he huffed out as he moved faster into her. She reached down with her right hand and massaged herself between her legs and his eyes were glued to them as he watched her work between their bodies. Her leg grew weak and he used the little strength he had left to prop them up, his orgasm rushing forward like a raging fire.

It happened so fast, he meant to pull out, but all of a sudden he was pulsing, and the tip of his cock was exploding into her body as she bit his shoulder and moaned while her orgasm flashed over her.

He let her leg drop to the floor so she could help him hold them up. Holding her close, he twisted to sit on the corner seat in his shower, bringing her to sit on his lap. His arms wrapped around her body and pulled her close to him, her head laid on his shoulder, her arms wrapped around him, both of them loathed to let go.

She sighed contentedly and he squeezed her to him.

His lips sought hers, softly, the urgency now sated, he loved how her lips molded to his. He loved how her body molded to his.

His lips trailed along her jaw, to her ear, his hand cupped the side of her face when he whispered, "I love you, Bridget Barnes, the Irish girl with copper hair."

She gasped or sobbed or something as she heard it again. A noise erupted from her throat and her arms tightened even tighter around his neck.

"I love you, Axel Dunbar, the badass with matáin."

His eyes watered. He'd try to tell himself it was water from the shower, but he knew better. She loved him and he loved her. They had a beautiful son and life was going to be very different from this point forward.

He sniffed, cleared his throat and asked, "What's matáin?"

51

Six months later

"Okay, that can go in the bedroom." Bridget directed traffic as the plethora of boxes, bags and furniture was brought into the house she and Axel bought and remodeled. Today was finally moving day. They'd been staying at the compound and she had to admit she felt safe there and as they remodeled this house, she was so grateful they had access to security professionals and equipment. Between each of the GHOST members they had a top-notch system in place and each of the members of GHOST signed off on approval of it.

Dodge walked in carrying Myles, Jax was right behind him carrying Maya. The babies were adorable with their mixed heritage coloring, big brown eyes and soft olive skin. They both smiled all the time and were happy.

"Where can we put these beasts where they won't get into trouble?"

Bridget laughed. "Will they be happier if they can look out the window? Put their pack and play by the front window."

Dodge handed her Myles, and she tickled his round belly which sent him into fits of laughter. Jax came forward and they hugged, with one arm, since each of them were holding a squirming six-month-old.

"The house looks great Bridget; you did a fantastic job with it."

"Thank you. We love it. How are you?"

"I'm fine. Only ten pounds to go to get back to my pre-baby weight. I never dreamed it would take so damned long.

Dodge walked to Jax and kissed her temple, "You are the most gorgeous woman in the world. Stop worrying about your weight."

Handing Myles to Jax, he lifted Maya from her arms and pretended Maya was flying to her pack and play, and she squealed in delight. He came to repeat the same for Myles and they all laughed.

"Mama will be in soon to watch over them, so put us to work please." Jax urged. "But, I'm going to kick Josh's ass for missing this to run off to a friend's wedding in Texas. I think he had this planned all along."

Bridget laughed. "How long will he be there?"

"I guess the entire week. Coward. Lazy coward."

Pilar walked in carrying a diaper bag. "Stop complaining about your brother. There's plenty of help here."

"Still gonna kick his ass. Just for old times' sake."

Pilar tsked and Bridget began directing traffic and issuing some directives.

Aidyn ran into the living room excited. "Momma, come and see, Daddy and Uncle Wyatt and Uncle Ford have my bed all set up."

He grabbed her hand and tugged her to his bedroom. The huge bunk bed set was a double bed on the bottom, with a staircase leading to the top bunk. Each step was a drawer so there was plenty of storage space.

Aidyn ran up the steps and flopped on the top bunk giggling. Wyatt and Ford laughed as they gathered the tools they'd used to set it up and watched Aidyn enjoying his new room.

Gaige, Sophie and Tate were in the spare bedroom setting up the bed in there, little Tate in a swing watching his Momma and Daddy work.

Lincoln, Skye, Megan and Shelby were in the kitchen moving boxes and unpacking and Bridget was trying to direct as much traffic as she could. Falcon Montgomery then walked in with another box and Bridget smiled. "That goes in the bedroom."

Falcon nodded and walked to the back of the house.

They'd found this great little house not far from Lynyrd Station on the Hill where Ford, Lincoln, Dodge and families all lived, and they jumped at the opportunity. They had loads of work to do on it, including a large addition, but it had come together beautifully. Bridget's mom had opted for a nice condo in town, not too far away, so Aidyn still had grandma close by. She'd also be babysitting again once Bridget had a new range set up.

The day flew by and between Pilar and Vivian the grandmas were kept very busy with five little ones running around. Axel grilled large steaks for everyone and much to Bridget's disgust, hot dogs for the littles as that's what they begged for. They found a spot to sit wherever they could. The kitchen and living room were open to each other so they could talk between the rooms.

Bridget sat on the fireplace hearth, which had been her dream item in the house. A gorgeous, stacked stone fireplace with a raised hearth so she could warm up on cool nights. Balancing her plate on her legs, she finished as much of her steak as she could. Taking a drink from her wine glass, Axel came and removed her plate from her legs and took it into the kitchen. He walked back into the living room and stood next to where she sat. Resting his hand on her shoulder, he said, "I'd like to make a toast."

She looked up at him and smiled.

"Thank you my friends, for all of your support, assistance and guidance as we closed out things in Steuben, bought this house and remodeled it and as we healed our family. We couldn't have done it without any of you and that is no lie."

They each drank to the toast. Axel dropped down beside her, tapped his glass to hers and said, "There's only one more thing that can make this complete." He pulled a small box from his pocket and opened it. "Bridget Barnes, will you become my wife? Will you marry me?"

Her eyes rounded; her jaw dropped. She was not expecting this. Her hands framed his face as she looked into his eyes. "Axel." She whispered because she had trouble getting the words out. She swallowed, "Axel. Yes. Yes."

He kissed her lips, then stood bringing her up with him. He slid the ring on her finger and turned to their friends.

"She said yes!"

They cheered and everyone tapped their glasses and snapped pictures as they celebrated the newly engaged couple of the day.

Gaige's phone rang and he stepped into the office around the corner.

When he came back out, he looked at Hawk and Falcon. "Josh needs some assistance in Texas, there's a situation."

***

You are cordially invited to attend Axel Dunbar and Bridget Barnes' wedding. To download your copy of Axel's Dream, click here - https://dl.bookfunnel.com/14qybyctpz

***

Keep Reading for a Sneak Peek at Defending Isabella

Straightening the bright green table cloth on one of the forty tables in the enormous backyard of her family's home, Isabella turns at the sound of a large vehicle rolling down the drive way.

Seeing a bus, which upon closer inspection, is the same bus her brother, Eric, left on last night for his bachelor party, pull down the driveway, her stomach twists. This is not good. He should have been home hours ago.

Emiliana, Isabella's sister walked to Isabella's side.

"This is not good Isi."

"I was just thinking the same thing. Where is momma?"

Both sisters turn toward the back doors perched atop a palatial stone patio to see their mother, Bianco, step out on the patio. The worry marring her beautiful face confirmed their suspicions.

The door to the bus opened and out stepped a group of men, most of them wobbling on their feet, with silly grins on their faces and their clothing in varying degrees of disarray.

Finally, after several unknown men stepped off the bus, a tall, broad shouldered man stepped off the bus, half carrying Eric.

The back door of the Martinez family home opened then slammed shut, Isabella's shoulders rose to her ears as she feared the glass on the custom oak doors would shatter at the impact.

Eric's bride...nope, Eric's very angry bride, Cecily Diaz, still not in her wedding dress, but wearing a white silken robe, her shiny dark hair perfectly coifed for her wedding ceremony, without the veil, her makeup impeccable, her tawny colored legs peeking from the slit in the robe with each giant step she took toward her future husband, if he lived that long, her white tennis shoes almost comical because they didn't fit the rest of the picture, and of course, if this wasn't so serious, marched toward the group of men.

"There she is boys..." Eric stuttered. "My beautiful bride." He managed to get out before Cecily let him have it.

Her fists were balled tightly at her sides and Isabella worried that she'd be patching up her brother before he made it to the alter today.

"You must have a death wish Eric Martinez. How dare you, on this day, our wedding day, disgrace me and my family and your own family by staying out all night, drinking and lord knows what else only to show up for our wedding four hours before hand drunk out of your mind."

Isabella walked forward, her sister Emiliana close behind her. "Cecily, let me take him in and get him cleaned up. It'll be alright."

"It won't be alright. Not now. He's ruined my perfect day. The day I've planned my ass off for. My parents, your parents, everyone, has been working on for a year."

Cecily turned back to Eric. "A fucking year!"

Isabella turned to her sister, "Emi, take Cecily back inside and let me deal with Eric."

Emi hesitantly approached Cecily, "Ceci, let's go and finish getting ready. Isi will take care of Eric. I promise it'll be alright."

Emi looked at her over Cecily's shoulder, hoping for an encouraging nod. Isabella gave it to her and was sending up silent prayers that she could sober her stupid brother out before the ceremony. It wasn't going to be easy though.

She approached Eric as the men largely either disbursed or some of them climbed back on the bus. She didn't know many of these men, which didn't surprise her, she'd lived in Texas for the past ten years, finishing medical school, then building her general practice in a small town just outside of Galveston.

The man holding Eric up, chuckled, "Why don't you point me in the direction you want him to go and I'll get him there for you. He's not very good on his feet right now."

"Why would you let him drink so much?"

"Look Princess, I had nothing to do with how much he drank. He was well on his way when I met him a few hours ago."

"You mean you just met him?"

"A few hours ago. He was celebrating pretty hard."

Shaking her head he walked to the other side of Eric, put her arm around his waist and tried hefting him off the big man hanging on to him. When she nearly dropped to her knees at Eric's weight, he looked over her brother's head at her and said, "Just point. I'll follow."

Taking a deep breath, she looked up to see Cecily standing on the patio watching them, Emi trying her hardest to get Cecily inside. Thinking it best to look like this would be doable, Isabella said, "Fine. Let's go in the side door, I'm afraid Cecily will stab him in the gut if he gets too close right now."

The larger man looked up at Cecily, then nodded. "Yep. She looks pretty pissed off."

He started walking with Eric stumbling alongside him and Isabella shook her head and took a mental inventory of the supplies she'd need to try and sober her brother out.

Cecily took two steps toward them as they walked past to the side door. "And another thing asshole, you won't be touching this..." She flung her robe open showing off her beautiful white lace teddy she'd purchased just for this night. "At all."

Emi grabbed the robe and pulled it closed, but Eric chose that moment to try and whistle. "Whoop, hot mama, here I come."

"Fucker." Cecily yelled just as Emi and her momma ushered her inside the house.

"Bud, you need to let her cool down before trying to be...whatever that was." The large man said to her brother.

Isabella looked over at him and half smiled. At least he was smart enough to know that much and sober enough to practically carry her stupid brother.

"My name's Josh."

***

Continue reading about Josh and Isabella, grab your copy here: Defending Isabella

Keep in touch and learn about new releases, sales, recipes, and other fun things by signing up for my newsletter - https://www.subscribepage.com/PJsReadersClub_copy

ALSO BY PJ FIALA

Click here to see a list of all of my books with the blurbs.

Contemporary Romance

Rolling Thunder Series

Moving to Love, Book 1

Moving to Hope, Book 2

Moving to Forever, Book 3

Moving to Desire, Book 4

Moving to You, Book 5

Moving Home, Book 6

Moving On, Book 7

Second Chances Series

Designing Samantha's Love, Book 1

Securing Kiera's Love, Book 2

Military Romantic Suspense

Bluegrass Security Series

Heart Thief, Book One

Finish Line, Book Two

Lethal Love, Book Three

Big 3 Security

Ford: Finding His Fire Book One

Lincoln: Finding His Mark Book Two

MEET PJ

Writing has been a desire my whole life. Once I found the courage to write, life changed for me in the most profound way. Bringing stories to readers that I'd enjoy reading and creating characters that are flawed, but lovable is such a joy.

When not writing, I'm with my family doing something fun. My husband, Gene, and I are bikers and enjoy riding to new locations, meeting new people and generally enjoying this fabulous country we live in.

I come from a family of veterans. My grandfather, father, brother, two sons, and one daughter-in-law are all veterans. Needless to say, I am proud to be an American and proud of the service my amazing family has given.

My online home is https://www.pjfiala.com.
You can connect with me on Facebook at https://www.facebook.com/PJFiala1,

and
Instagram at https://www.Instagram.com/PJFiala.
If you prefer to email, go ahead, I'll respond -
pjfiala@pjfiala.com.

Made in the USA
Monee, IL
09 September 2022

13662047R00184